Glass Ceiling

by

Evadeen Brickwood

Episode 4

EVADEEN BRICKWOOD

"Glass Ceiling"

This book was first published in paperback by
Evadeen Brickwood on KDP Amazon

Find this book in digital format also at:
Kindle Store, Smashwords, Neobooks and Tolino

First edition 2021 by Evadeen Brickwood on KDP Amazon

Amazon Print ASIN:
Amazon ISBN: 9798716112094
NLSA ISBN: 9781049206196

Cover Design by Birgit Böttner
Image Source: Pixabay
Book Layout: Birgit Böttner
Marketing: Alphalogic International

Charlie Proudfoot would rather not get involved in solving murders, but her friend Lerato Gwala, a private detective from Johannesburg, believes that Charlie's talent of intuition will give her murder investigations the edge. So Charlie agrees to help Lerato with just one more case.

In this Episode:

Judith Holland is overjoyed when she lands her
dream job with a large pharmaceutical company
in Johannesburg.
Then a colleague is found stabbed to death and
fear grips the accountant.
When more bodies are turning up, the question
on everybody's mind is: Who will be next?

<u>Other Titles by Evadeen Brickwood</u>

In the time travel youth series:

"Children of the Moon" ("Remember the Future 1")

"The Speaking Stone of Caradoc" ("Remember the Future 2")

"The Secret of the Bird God" ("Remember the Future 3")

in the German Edition:

"Kinder des Mondes" ("Erinnerung an die Zukunft 1")

Novels:

"A Half Moon Adventure" (An Adventure Mystery)

"Abenteuer Halbmond" (German Edition)

"Singing Lizards" (A Mystery-Adventure set in Africa)

"Singende Eidechsen" (German edition)

"The Rhino Whisperer" (A Crime Mystery)

"Der Nashorn Flüsterer" (German edition)

Other Titles by Evadeen Brickwood

In the Charlie Proudfoot series so far:

1) A Hazy Shade of Murder

2) Claws Out

3) It Could Have Been Love

Special Thanks and Acknowledgements

I'd like to thank Franciska Griesel for enlightening me with her knowledge on the subject of accounting. I hope I did the information she gave me justice. Christian Grosch for stepping up when power outages in our area threatened to sabotage the completion of this book and all my test readers.

For Franciska

Chapter ONE

Judith tried to control her frenzied breathing and pressed her back against the house wall. She listened. How long had she been standing there by the rough, cold wall, trying to make herself invisible? Had it been five minutes or ten? A security door opened then slammed closed with a loud creak and a thud.

Somebody hurried toward the street with long, heavy strides down the paving around the corner. It was a man by the sound of it, but how could she be sure? Was it him? She heard beeping as the car unlocked then a car door opened.

She stood stock-still, scared half to death, her heart thumping hard against her chest, her breathing more shallow now, calming down.

Had he seen her, the man in the street?

He'd walked out of the building she had just fled. The man must be living in one of the apartments, or visiting - or was it – him? Would he come back and check where she had gone? She moved away from the wall just a tiny bit to catch a glimpse, but all she could see were cars parked in the street. Judith could only hope that the untidy stretch of grass next to the house wall didn't give away the clicking of her heels. She wanted to be invisible, inaudible.

To manage a clear thought was immensely difficult. Panic, panic, panic.

From the corner of her eye, Judith saw the body still lying on the tiny lawn behind the apartment building, right between the washing line and a bumpy footpath. Just a few feet away from the washing line. It was slumped to one side – the body – almost sitting up the end of the bumpy footpath. It wasn't that far from her

The blood from the back wound was no longer spurting out as before. It had subsided into a mere trickle since Judith had run away from the body in terror. She held her cardigan closed, where the blood had stained her dress. It was obvious that the person on the grass had been stabbed in the back. The red hilt of a kitchen knife was protruding from the casual blue shirt the woman was wearing, the blade all the way inside the wound.

The bulk was that of a blonde woman. A short, stocky woman with her red-stained hair all in a mess, hiding a plump face, framing the red hilt in her upper body like a piece of art. She was no longer alive, the woman with the knife in her back.

Judith felt a sense of panic rise again in her throat, but she couldn't scream. Only a soundless moan escaped her lips as she exhaled. She bit on her hand hard to stop the urge. *Slowly*, she reminded herself. Breathe *slowly*.

Daylight was fading fast.

The ugly sight of the dead body felt to Judith like a punch in the stomach, but she couldn't look away as if to make sure that the body wouldn't disappear or reawaken. What if Hannah was still alive? Yes, she knew the woman in the grotesque pose on the ground by the washing line. She squinted into the growing darkness, but all she could make out was the blonde hair hanging down Hannah's back, hiding her face.

There was no movement. Judith took a few measured breaths. It was too late. The woman would not come back to life. Oh, why was this happening?

The thought didn't feel as bad as before, when she had fled from the scene to the house wall, scared that he might find her. That man she had seen earlier when she'd arrived at her colleague's apartment to discuss the last-minute paperwork. They were accountants and worked at the same company. She still clutched her bag with the papers she was meant to give to her colleague.

Again, Judith listened intently, but there was no sound in the street now. She sighed and pressed herself against the wall again. Just in case.

He'd seemed nervous or upset - the man. Walking so fast. Where was he going in his car? Never mind – as long as he left her alone. She just remembered seeing a man's trouser leg and Nike shoe before he swiftly closed his apartment door behind him. Earlier. Two doors down from Hannah's apartment.

Judith suddenly could no longer think of her name. The name of the body by the washing line. What was wrong with her mind? Wait… it was Hannah. That's right, her name was Hannah Bradlow. It was Hannah, who was lying there in the damp grass.

Had she died instantly or had she suffered? The

thought surprised her. *Pull yourself together!* She scolded herself. She shouldn't be thinking thoughts like that or they would drive her mad. She should get out of here – and quickly. This place wasn't safe.

What time was it? How long had she been standing there by the wall?

The question was compelling and took the lead in her head, but Judith Holland still didn't have an answer. Did it matter? She just needed to get home. Home was safe. There she could sort out the mess in her head. The shock.

David was coming to visit tonight.

He'd be there any moment now… and she couldn't tell anybody of this... this… thing she had witnessed. Least of all David.

Even calling the police was out of the question. They would never believe her. She'd babble about spurting blood, a knife and that she knew the dead woman. They would take her into custody for sure. That's all she needed!

David. Her breathing slowed at last as she thought of David. If she didn't get to her apartment soon, he might already be there waiting - and she needed to get out of her dress. Shower, then new clothes and calm her nerves.

She noticed the blue flicker of TV screens behind curtained windows. They were surely watching the popular TV show she had wanted to watch as well tonight before David came to visit. At what time was it on? She couldn't remember. Her thoughts began to scramble again. How long should she wait before walking into the street? What was the man doing in his car? Was he waiting for her to come out of hiding?

A car engine roared and a gear slammed into position.

She could only guess that it was the man, who had rushed out of the house and into the street. A quick revving of the engine and then a metallic purring sound. Tyres plopped off the pavement and onto the tar. She felt relief as the car pulled off from the curb. The man who lived in the apartment building was leaving! Gone. He would not come back for her. She was safe now – or was she?

The fear in her mouth tasted dry and metallic. She could finally leave.

For a heart-stopping moment, she paused.

Somewhere above, a woman yelled shrill insults and a man answered angrily. It must be in one of the apartments in one of the buildings! Judith held her breath and tried not to listen to the words. Only one word stood out… bitch. Bitch, bitch, bitch. An ugly word!

She didn't want to be seen. If they saw her, they would think that she might have something to do with this, this... She couldn't be seen near a dead body. It would make her life impossible. If somebody saw her and called the police, she would be in trouble for being even near a dead body.

They hadn't been on the best of terms, her and Hannah, but she felt sorry for Hannah Bradlow now. Sorry that she had to die like this, but Judith had to think of herself now. She had to get out of this place. Should she just run away from all the prying eyes? A window slammed closed. Then another one. She could no longer hear the fight between the man and the woman. The word that greatly troubled her still resounded in her head: bitch, bitch, bitch.

I must get home… Judith thought decisively. She needed to take action.

She peeled herself off the cold wall, took a deep

breath and walked casually into the street, holding her head down, clutching her bag against her body, while holding her cardigan closed in front. No scarf or hat or collar to hide behind.

Her car was parked on the other side of the road. They didn't have security guards here, but cameras, maybe. Casual, she reminded herself. Act as if you live here or were just visiting.

She needed to get home. Home. It wasn't much of a home, her apartment. The temporary apartment she'd occupied since moving to Johannesburg. Her boyfriend David came as often as he could to visit from Pretoria. The dear. Her company was paying for the small apartment two suburbs away from work only until the end of January. She had the whole of January to find a bigger place. On her new salary, that wouldn't be too difficult.

She'd only lived in Johannesburg for a few months, but it seemed like ages without him. Judith hadn't seen him for two weeks. She understood that he had his job to think about and he couldn't drive back to Pretoria every morning. It was a long drive and his job was important.

Only a few more steps to the unimpressive olive-coloured Ford now.

Judith pressed the button of her remote. Lights flashed and the beeping was too loud! She jumped inside her skin, but nobody seemed to care. She was nearly there.

With the grand salary she was paid at the new company, she'd also be able to afford a better car in no time. She opened the door and threw her bag on the passenger seat.

Just as she put the key into the ignition, a window upstairs was ripped open again and loud angry voices reached her even inside the car. Bitch, bitch, bitch!

Judith started the car and fled.

In no time, she was down the road, farther and farther away from this awful place. She trembled each time the traffic lights changed to red – not daring to jump the light, trying to be patient, steadily moving away from that cursed apartment building in Killarney and the still, blue bulk with the messy blonde hair.

David had said on the phone that he wanted to talk to her about something, but now there was none of the happy flutters she'd felt before.

There were a number of things he might want to talk to her about. Was he coming to live with her in Johannesburg or would he... propose? The happy flutters returned for a second. If he did she'd allow him to do the thing he liked so much... come on, traffic light! Her thoughts were getting all tangled up again. A proposal, that's what she wanted more than anything, but not on a day like this. Why not?

This was as good as any day. What if he did propose? That's what she had wanted more than anything for a long time but she was not in the right frame of mind for a proposal. No way could she deal with happy feelings now. And then again, she'd been hoping for a while now – for David to put a ring on it. After two years of dating. Maybe he would finally pay her back the loan she'd given him without asking questions six months ago.

Her thoughts went round and round again and she nearly hit the food delivery bike as she turned. The guy on the bike hooted angrily. She still saw Hannah's body on the grass by the apartment building, could still feel the fear and her heart began to thump.

How could she keep something like that a secret? Especially from David.

Music would help! She turned on the car radio. The news were on. Alright then, anything was better than her own thoughts. She didn't listen to the news or the music after the news, but she made it back home in one piece.

Maybe she and David could find a place of their own together and if they were getting married... *Don't get ahead of yourself*, the sober accountant said to the giddy girlfriend inside of her.

Her head was hurting by the time she arrived home. Judith parked her car and dragged herself up the stairs. In the bedroom, she took her clothes off, put them into a plastic bag and deposited the bag in the kitchen. If she had the time, the bag would disappear in the dumpster downstairs tonight. She took two painkillers and her pumping headache faded. After her shower, she felt better, put on her flowery shirt that David liked so much and threw the plastic bag into the trash downstairs. Three of her problems were solved.

She lit the three large candles in the lounge and prepared some food in the tiny kitchen. Slowly the image of the dead body also faded. She'd be okay.

It was a stroke of luck that David arrived later than expected.

He had to put in overtime right now and – truth be told – was not keen to make the drive to Johannesburg and face his girlfriend. He'd sent her a message before he got into the car, so she wouldn't worry. Nothing out of the ordinary, then. Work came before her - as usual. That's how it should be, shouldn't it?

By the time he'd made his way through traffic and rang the bell at her Linden apartment, Judith was in an almost cheerful state of mind.

"Hi liefling," she greeted David and took the chicken & mushroom pies out of the microwave. The bowl with the mixed salad was already on the table. The candles created a romantic atmosphere and soothing music surrounded them as he stepped into the sparsely furnished lounge. David was a regular-looking guy about the same height as Judith with short brown hair. He had quickly changed into a clean shirt and pants, but as so often, he still smelled of work. Judith didn't mind.

"Hi there, I'm sorry I'm so late. Traffic was a bitch," he said and gave her a kiss on the forehead. It was not exactly a romantic gesture. Bitch, bitch, bitch…

"It's okay, love. Are you hungry?" Judith placed the pies on plates and pushed back her nervousness deep down to the pit of her stomach. Everything was okay now.

"Starving," David said. He sat down and began to eat. She thought that champagne would go nicely with the food, should he truly propose.

"You like it? Sorry, there was no time to cook. I hope it's alright."

"Just fine. Can I have some coke?" David helped himself to the salad. Well, he couldn't expect a feast, considering the circumstances. It was chicken and mushroom pie. Judith knew that his favourite pie was pepper steak. Could she sense what was coming?

It was time for David to tell her his news - and it wasn't a proposal. He would also not be moving to Joburg any time soon. Judith sat rigid and upright on her chair. Not good news, but at least it was out.

Phew. The level-headed part of her was relieved.

No telling how she would have reacted with her nerves still tingling from the harrowing experience she'd gone through today. Yet she was crying on the inside, while he kept talking.

David would be moving. He had decided to emigrate. To New Zealand and soon. What, New Zealand?! Her heart sank.

Thankfully, Judith managed not to burst out in tears. David had been made a job offer and had until Monday to decide. He was an electrician of the highest order and sought after in the field. The company he'd been working for these last 5 years needed somebody at their Wellington dealership.

New Zealand? Judith struggled to take in the news… she felt overwhelmed.

There was a tightness in her chest and she heard the pumping of her own heart right in her ears. It was getting louder, drowning out the music and David's voice.

"Judith? Judith… I asked you something."

Her thoughts returned to the table in her apartment with David. His face looked puzzled.

"Yes, David?" Her hands felt a little warmer as she

leaned back. He'd already asked her to take care of his cat. He could hardly take her with him to New Zealand and nobody in Pretoria wanted to adopt her.

"I asked you if you could get Dani a holiday job at your company."

"What? A holiday job?" He hadn't broken up with her – yet. So it was probably alright to ask Charmaine in HR if they needed students for the holiday season.

Dani was David's sister. She studied in Johannesburg to become a beautician. A temp job at a pharmaceutical company would surely look good on her CV.

"Yes, I guess, I can ask HR."

But David wasn't done talking yet. He talked and talked and she only half-listened. The loan he was supposed to pay back wasn't even mentioned and she was too shocked at his news to broach the subject. She needed the money back. It was Christmas and it would also pay toward a deposit on the new apartment. Would she need a new apartment now that she was all on her own?

She saw the knife next to her plate with the half-eaten chicken pie and saw the slumped over body with the knife stuck in her back and blonde hair framing the red hilt of the knife.

David liked blonde women. Long hair. Judith, on the other hand, was a little on the fuller side with a big bum and dark wavy hair that hung over her shoulders. She was intelligent and nice enough, but she wished she could be more attractive for David. More the way he liked women to be. She tried to concentrate on what David was saying.

Her mind obeyed when she resolutely chased the nightmarish image of the dead body away. At least for now.

She even smiled while David blathered on about the new position in Wellington he would have, his new responsibilities and how much more they were offering him if he took the job.

"South Africa is becoming so bad," he said. "All that crime and load-shedding. Half the time, we don't even have electricity. New Zealand is the chance of a lifetime."

It was time for him to make a move abroad like all the other sensible young people David knew. So many of them were emigrating. Judith nodded then roused herself.

"What about me?" she asked.

The question cut through his elated mood like a hot knife through butter.

"Babes, I can't think about that now. They only told me today about this," he answered. "And you just started a new job in Joburg. Isn't that exactly what you wanted?"

What he didn't say was that he'd heard a rumour about Judith. It bothered him, although it must have been a while ago when it happened. She was damaged goods. Since he'd heard about it from a friend, he couldn't see himself marrying her anymore. He could do better for sure. Instead of asking her outright, he made it sound as if it was her choice not to join him abroad.

"You're making so much money here. It's your career. I can't expect you to leave all that behind and move to New Zealand with me." It seemed like a logical reason.

"So you want to break up with me?"

If she was honest with herself, this had been one of the possibilities playing on her mind when David had told her about the 'big thing' he wanted to discuss with her. Judith was so used to not confronting issues and glossing over everything unpleasant and always being agreeable – that she couldn't remember how to be honest with herself. But she was gutted at the prospect.

How much worse could this day get? She closed her eyes and took a deep breath, not wanting to hear the answer David would surely hurtle in her direction. She made a fist with her right hand and braced herself.

"No, no of course not," David was quick to calm her down. Was he being truthful? Judith couldn't say for sure. Especially not after the day she'd had. And yet, she couldn't tell him about Hannah, couldn't open up. Especially not now.

"Then how's this going to work?" Judith tried to keep her voice steady. "A long-distance relationship with you in Wellington and me being here in Joburg? So far? That's never going to work. It didn't work for JP and Lizelle and they were both in South Africa."

He touched her arm, but she shook off his hand. That was all she dared to do to show how displeased she was.

"Don't say that…" He could hardly say what was

really on his mind. Letting her down easy was not as easy as his brother had made it out to be. *Lie to her a little bit, pretend. Women can have such tempers*, he had told him. And there was still the small issue of Dani's holiday job. She needed credits for her beautician's certificate.

'Cry Me A River…' How ironic that this song should play just now. Judith got up and switched the radio off. Any kind of music got on her nerves. She mustn't lose her head now. Judith's smile didn't reach her eyes, but David was oblivious to the state she was in. She was rarely in a bad mood. Always so agreeable that it was almost boring.

"Why are you so touchy tonight?" He asked her. "We'll work it out somehow."

His tone betrayed what he was really thinking.

"Oh yes, how? I don't care where I work, as long as we can be together." Judith's voice trembled. "When are you planning to go?"

It wasn't lost on David that her smile disappeared for a moment. Oh, it was so difficult to say no to her.

"Whenever I'm ready," he snapped then thought better of it. "Sorry. This is all very new for me. Let me go and check things out over there before we talk about you coming over. How does that sound?"

In reality, their relationship had run its course and David was itching for change and to take on a new challenge. He had no intentions of asking Judith to come and join him in Wellington, but it would be best to pretend a little while longer. Just tonight, she was not as easy to talk to. She was more prickly than usual and put him on the spot. It felt rather uncomfortable.

"I don't know why you're not asking me to come with you, to marry you and start a new life in New Zealand together. Wouldn't that be better than all this waiting around? With my training, I can find a good job in Wellington, I'm sure."

"Let's not rush things…" David was evasive and his eyes darted around. *What's wrong with her tonight?* He thought helplessly. *She normally backs down quite quickly.* He'd tell his brother off for sure for giving him bad advice.

"Rush things? We've been together for two years. Don't you think it's time to go to the next level?" Judith insisted. Feeling dizzy from showing this courage she was not accustomed to. It was as if her voice was taking on a life of its own.

Oh, these career-women, David groaned on the inside, echoing his brother's sentiment. *Always wanting things to go their way.*

Of course, he couldn't tell her about the woman he'd met last month at a braai in Pretoria. Irma Boshoff. Their parents were friends and introduced them to each other. He barely remembered her from way back when they'd played in her parents' garden. Irma had grown into a looker with long blonde hair and a killer figure. She taught Life Sciences at an Afrikaans school, but having a career was not as important to her as it was to Judith.

His brother was right: Irma would be a much better fit for him in the long run. Especially now that he'd been told about Judith's past. She would do as his side chick until he left, but Irma was marriage material.

But instead of confessing his true feelings, David had chosen not to share them with Judith. Despite this, he bristled at his girlfriend's unexpected reaction.

"Have you been talking to your mother again?" His tone was condescending. "I just told you, it will happen when I'm ready. Rushing into things like that… you know… that's never a good idea."

Judith felt immediately self-conscious. Her mother was a simple woman, who had brought up three children on her own when her husband left her for another woman he'd met at work. People had blamed her, of course. The siblings had always been clean and fed, but there had never been money for luxuries and the children were a constant reminder of her failure to hold onto her husband.

"So, you'd rush into moving to another country… another continent, but not making things official with me?"

David had to admit that she had a point there.

Judith was clever and David had a hard time wriggling his way out of this one. They argued forth and back for another hour, while the salad wilted on their plates.

This was their first real fight.

She had always avoided confrontations with David and rather tried to please him as best as she could. Her nerves were raw, but it didn't make Judith feel any better to speak her mind. She was out of her depth when it came to feelings. Had she been too forward? This relationship was important to Judith and marriage would add tremendous value to her social standing. Should she share today's events with David?

No, she couldn't go that far. He might be shocked. Would he leave her like her father had left their mother? She couldn't take that chance. The tiny chance she still had.

Judith tossed and turned for hours that night, while David slept on the couch.

All she wanted was to draw a line under the worst day of her life, yet the day wouldn't end. Her thoughts went round and round in her head. Confusing thoughts, scary thoughts.

Eventually, she fell into an uneasy sleep. She had managed to convince herself that all was not lost, that there was still hope. David hadn't said NO to getting married or to her joining him in New Zealand. He just didn't want to rush into things. Maybe she should take his word for it?

Her murdered colleague was no longer foremost on her mind. She wanted to get married and be with

David, wherever he was going.

When she finally nodded off to sleep, she dreamed of their wedding venue in the nature reserve she'd earmarked about a year ago, when she'd paged through a bridal magazine. It was affordable and just the right size, the venue. It wasn't a big wedding in her dream. Just family and a few friends.

She was wearing the off-the-shoulder fishtail dress she had admired in the magazine and had the most beautiful diamond ring on her finger and she felt beautiful.

David looked into her eyes with love and pride as he slipped on the golden wedding band. Everyone at the reception laughed happily. They danced and danced the night away. Judith felt so good.

At least in her dream, David was showing commitment and devotion.

Chapter TWO

Three weeks earlier, at the beginning of November, things couldn't have been more perfect for Judith Holland. She had started her new job as an accountant with one of the largest pharmaceutical companies in the country. An international company. It was a dream job after years of studies and the first job after her articles that hadn't lasted very long.

MultoPharm's Johannesburg branch was not very big. Not even fifty employees. Most of these employees were now sitting around a large conference table.

During the weekly staff meeting, she would be introduced to her new colleagues and she wanted to make a good impression.

Judith was sitting at the lower end of the massive conference table, studded with centrepieces of red poinsettias and silver stars and baubles, listening to one item of the agenda after another, trying to react to curious looks in her direction with a simple smile.

She had chosen an unremarkable olive-green shift dress this morning. At the last minute, she'd decided against a more formal suit. Standing out on her first day, was the last thing she wanted. It had been a good choice. She was surprised at the fairly casual dress code, so different to her old company's. Even the top boss wore a simple polo shirt and shorts.

The local CEO of the MultoPharm Corporation checked his wristwatch. The monthly meeting at the company's branch office in Johannesburg was drawing to an end. Only forty two employees were in attendance. According to their head office in Frankfurt, these compulsory meetings were part of a very necessary teambuilding process.

In his own opinion, John Buitendacht thought this was an over-the-top modern approach, but it was part of his job to keep up appearances and he was determined to follow the directives of the German parent company to the letter.

Buitendacht had given the assembly good news and bad news and observed how Julius Mandel, the head of MultoPharm's legal department, had fallen asleep for a few minutes. Perhaps he was working him too hard, but heck, what did he pay him all that money for? If they lost the current court case, the branch in South Africa could pack it in.

He'd reached the second last item on the agenda. It was the action cricket team's dismal performance at last week's tournament where they'd faced one of their supplier firm's team. Positive spin... positive spin... he reminded himself as so often, pushing his rather competitive nature back.

The Olsen Limited players had done a great job and won by thirty two runs. A whitewash by his standards, but John Buitendacht had thought of some encouraging platitudes in the name of the all-important team spirit.

"I expect our team to whip the Olsens at the next innings..." Some people clapped and someone whistled. "You can do it!"

"We're playing Tomko International next time," Mathilda Mayer, his PA, whispered. "On the 14th of December."

"I mean, Tomko International. I hear they're sissies." More clapping. "So keep up your efforts and good luck to our team. Training, training, training." The CEO gave a little cough. "Let's win this tournament!"

"We only have three more training sessions left," Miss Mayer said. "It's almost Christmas time, sir."

John Buitendacht looked at her slightly annoyed. He couldn't be expected to remember all these details. Then his stance softened. What would he do without his private secretary? Mathilda was indeed irreplaceable, but this meeting was dragging on. With some luck - if there was no further holdup - he would make it for lunch with his golf buddies in Houghton and at least one round of golf and lunch before the conference call in the afternoon.

"Hmm yeah, well do your best…" he said in conclusion. "Last point on the agenda…." His PA pushed a note in front of him. "Wait… our office angel Mathilda sent flowers and a greeting card to Nomsa Pretorius on the birth of her bundle of joy… on the 17th of last month." He read his notes. "I believe Nomsa and her husband welcomed a strapping boy by the name of Oliver. I hope you all signed the greeting card."

Mathilda Mayer nodded silently. He knew that she considered it her job to make sure of such things.

"And last but not least, we have new additions to our own family here at MultoPharm. Say hello to our new security guard… Herbert Tuins…" A slightly scrawny, friendly-looking fellow stood up and gave a slight bow. "… and Judith Holland, who will reinforce our troops at the accounts department. Wynand, you must be so pleased. I hear that Judith worked as an auditor with KYMP. Very impressive, indeed. A cordial welcome to both of you. I hope you will be with us for a long time to come." Wynand Ryker, the chief accountant, gestured toward Judith. He motioned for her to stand up.

Judith saw it from the corner of her eye. She had been looking out of the enormous tinted windows of the conference room, admiring the willow trees in the park-like grounds she was planning to explore later. Her mind had wandered from the point when Mr. Buitendacht had given them the sales figures for the last quarter and praised employees she had yet to meet. When she heard her name mentioned and saw her new boss gesturing, she roused herself and stood up, taking care not to tip over her water glass in the process. She could be so clumsy, sometimes.

Again, Judith smiled at as many colleagues as possible, not consciously seeing their faces. Something she had learned during the three-day assertiveness course her last company had sent her on. Success. People seemed to be smiling back.

Herbert, the new security guard had introduced himself when she arrived for work this morning. He was a nice enough fellow; very polite and efficient. She had listened to a guided meditation in the car to calm her nerves and convinced herself that everything would be just fine.

'I am cool, calm and collected…' she repeated in her mind.

The company *family* clapped for a little while. Herbert Tuins seemed to enjoy the brief attention, while Judith couldn't wait to meet her new colleagues at the accounts department.

She had met Wynand Ryker, the Chief Financial Officer, only shortly before the meeting. He had shaken her hand at the reception and ordered one of the admin staff to take Judith under her wings. She had been processed for half an hour. The secretary had given MultoPharm's newest accountant an access card with her picture fastened to a band in the company colours to wear it around her neck.

The card was needed to open most doors and a few cupboards, but the secretary spoke too fast for Judith to remember all the details. No problem, she would ask later.

Would her new colleagues in the Finance Department readily accept her? Her last job at KYMP had ended dismally in her resignation two months into her contract. The office bitch had made her life miserable and even though Judith had complained to HR, nothing at all had been done about the situation.

She had high hopes that in a company like MultoPharm, things would be better.

It would be fantastic if a promotion was on the cards in a few months.

Judith peeped through the security glass window of the office door on the third floor of the building, where she'd been told to report for work.

She couldn't see much as the angle of the sun blinded her and took a deep breath before she used her new access card to open the heavy door to the office that would be her new professional home.

She pushed it open with her shoulder just underneath the little security glass window, while balancing two folders in the crook of her elbow, and entered the office.

As she closed the door with her back, she could make out seven desks with widescreen monitors in the room. To her great delight, Judith saw that the entire wall facing her was a window front made of the same tinted glass she had seen in the conference room during the meeting. Wonderful. Natural light flooded the room. This was a big plus compared to the artificial light she had endured at her last job.

Where was her desk? None of the heads that were bent over piles of documents behind the computer screens moved up to greet her. That wasn't unusual. In her experience, accountants were generally not the most sociable of people.

"Harrumph. Hello…" she tried a little nervously.

Judith cleared her throat and her new boss, who had told her to stand up at the staff meeting, looked up and pushed back his chair. He seemed friendly enough. Judith didn't recognise any of the other faces but presumed that most of the people in this office had also been present.

Wynand Ryker's large desk was right next to the enormous window, facing the opposite direction of all the other desks, just like a school teacher's at the front of a classroom. It was a large desk with a whiteboard next to it. Something was scribbled on the whiteboard, but Judith didn't pay attention to the writing. It was more important to make a good impression now.

The castors of Wynand Ryker's chair scraped over the rough carpet squares and the chair squeaked when he stood up. Yes, that chair was definitely noisy.

A few faces popped up and observed the unfolding scene. Judith tried to smile in the general direction of the room, but it was hard to tell if anyone looked at her or smiled back. She pushed her glasses up onto the top of her head with one hand and clutched the two folders tightly with the other.

"Hello," she repeated.

Mr. Ryker was in his forties, tall with surprisingly dark, curly hair. He moved toward her with arms outstretched. This was a little over the top, but Judith shifted the cardboard folders into the crook of her left elbow and Wynand Ryker grabbed her now free hand and shook it vigorously.

Had it not been for his pale complexion and expressionless face, he could have been called handsome. He had taken off his jacket and she could smell his deodorant. It was the same musky deodorant her boyfriend David used. Strangely, the scent comforted her in this somewhat uncomfortable situation.

"Hello again, Ms Holland. I'm Wynand Ryker," he introduced himself again quite unnecessarily. "Head of the Finance Department. We saw each other earlier this morning."

Did he think, she wouldn't remember? *Cool, calm and collected.* Judith repeated the mantra from the podcast she had listened to while driving to work.

"Yes, that's right," she said brightly. "I remember. I'm Judith, your new subject." She smiled and bowed slightly, but was unsure if Wynand Ryker had understood her little joke. Accountants weren't known for their sense of humour, but perhaps this apparently friendly man would be the exception.

He didn't react at all and withdrew his hand. "Well, let's do the proper introductions around here, then." He turned to address her new colleagues, who tried to appear not too curious. "Everybody listen up…"

There were the faces again. Judith counted five.

"… for those, who weren't at the meeting this morning… this is Judith…"

"Holland," Judith anticipated what he was going to say. *Cool, calm and collected*, she reminded herself.

"Judith Holland. As you know she's replacing Waldemar. Come, come closer and greet her personally. There you go." He waved for his 'subjects' to approach.

A choir of chairs scraped over the carpet tiles and her new colleagues joined them. Most of them wore glasses, which was to be expected. Two accountants stayed in their chairs and just lifted their hands in greeting. Mr. Ryker pointed to them and gave her the names, but Judith had already forgotten them the very next moment.

"… and Hannah Bradlow sits over there." Her boss pointed to a chubby, blonde woman in a stiff, light blue dress, who nodded in greeting before standing up to leave the office. Judith lifted her hand and waved uneasily. One of the colleagues, who had come forward to greet her, extended his hand.

"Hi, I'm Anthony Sedibe. You can call me Tony. Welcome in the dungeon." It was supposed to be a joke. A bad one that reminded her of her previous job.

"Hi Tony, thank you. I'm Judith."

She smiled and shook his and everybody else's hand. Apart from Tony, there were Charmaine Trichardt, Elizabeth Brody and Noni Mabitsela, who stood in a half-circle around her. In Judith's opinion, accountants were not renowned for being great conversationalists either, but at least they were trying.

"Don't let me keep you from your calculations. I'm sure we'll catch up later. Over lunch, perhaps," she said brightly and everybody returned to their desks, obviously relieved that the awkward introductions were over. Wynand Ryker took Judith by the arm and was about to show her to her desk when the heavy office door flew open.

A balding, middle-aged man walked in with an imperious gait, waving sheets of paper dramatically over his head. "Wynand, I must speak to you about this," he complained. "I thought it was taken care of."

He slapped the paper sheets onto the large desk in the front with an indignant expression on his face.

"Not now, Julius," her new boss tried to say calmly. "We are busy welcoming our new colleague to the gang."

The man, called Julius, looked Judith up and down. It was not a very friendly look and she thought it was better to stare at her shoes. Pumps that matched the colour of her skirt suit. Of course, she had seen the man at the staff meeting as well. He had fallen asleep for a bit, which some of the colleagues had found amusing.

"Right, sorry," Julius Mandel said impatiently, remembering his manners, and Judith felt his boring eyes on her and she looked up at him. "Send Hannah over, then. Asap."

"Yes, as soon as she's back from her meeting."

"Of course, she's in a meeting," the lawyer moaned.

"Don't be such an ogre!" Wynand Ryker scolded him. "Say hello to Judith Holland."

"Judith, this is the manager of our legal department, Julius Mandel."

"Please to meet you, sir," she said, trying not to meet his eyes. Perhaps he would forget that she existed if she appeared small and boring.

"Right. Sorry, pleased to meet you," the man said and they shook hands. The polite moment didn't last long. "Wynand, I need to speak to Hannah as soon as possible." Julius Mandel turned around and strode back to the door. "I left the paperwork here. Tell her to go over the figures again." he pointed to the sheets of paper on the large desk.

"Yes, I'll do that," Wynand Ryker said in a slightly annoyed tone and Julius Mandel left the room. He turned back to Judith and guided her to the desk farthest at the back.

"We are training for the action cricket tournament tonight. Twice a week actually," Wynand Ryker told her. "It would be great if you could join the team."

Andy interrupted. "Waldemar played on the team. Only if you're interested, of course. We'll meet in the parking lot after work. The company's minibus takes us to the courts in Marlboro and back here, so we don't have to all drive and wait around."

Wynand Ryker nodded and looked at Judith.

She pondered this for a split second. Her boyfriend David was more of a rugby-man like most guys she knew in Pretoria, so she wasn't too familiar with the sport of cricket. Judith had played netball at school and been to a couple of cricket matches at the stadium in Centurion. That was it. Playing cricket was a different ball game altogether and she would probably embarrass herself.

"That would be splendid. Yes, of course, I'll play for the team." She gave her boss a radiant smile.

Actually, she didn't like sports in general and the little apartment she'd moved into needed a bit of tending to. She had planned to unpack her kitchen stuff that was still in cardboard boxes on the floor. On the other hand, she knew full well that this little sacrifice was expected of her and would make her transition into the select club of accountants at the Finance Office so much easier.

"Great." Her new boss seemed delighted. "That makes four from our department then. Anthony, Elizabeth, you and myself."

"Splendid," Judith repeated. She didn't know what else to say about being inducted into the action cricket team.

She put her folders onto the desk. It was time to focus on work. From here, Judith had a view of the company gardens. Well, at least the treetops and a flower-framed lawn in the distance. The tree's long leafy tendrils moved gently in the breeze as if to welcome her. They were on the third floor after all and outside the window, was the tall willow tree she had noticed between the entrance and the main parking lot.

The grandiose covered entrance and the reception area had to be just below this office. The view of the garden made up for the ugly office buildings all around them.

On her first day at work, Judith received lessons in the usage of internal software and procedures. Not that it differed much from the software she'd used at her previous job at KYMP, but she tried to pay attention nonetheless.

Work began to feel familiar to Judith Holland and she began to relax. She had a good feeling about this new job and if she was anything, it was competent. Here, she wouldn't have to put up with snarky Helene and Mahendra's bullying.

This job was a godsend. If David decided to join her in Johannesburg, her life would be perfect. Before long, they'd save up for the deposit on a house in the suburbs and then they would get married and have children. Judith's thoughts drifted into a happy future.

Life was good to her at last.

*

Meanwhile, the cricket match around her picked up again.

"Look out!" Elizabeth Brody couldn't help yelling.

A red cricket ball swished past Judith's head and she managed to duck just in time. It wasn't the first time she would miss a catch.

"Hey, be careful!" One of the technicians from the fourth floor yelled. "Don't break her. We need this one on our team. Here, let me give you a hand. You don't have much experience with action cricket, do you?"

"You got me there." Judith took a deep breath and adjusted her helmet.

It had been a few weeks since her first day at work and Judith had become part of the MultoPharm family. Today they were practising for the last time before the Christmas holidays and the last match of the year was scheduled for Saturday morning. Judith was terrified of letting her team down, but what choice did she have? She was looking forward to the Christmas party straight after the match. There would be a braai and dancing at the company. Some cheer at the end of the year.

Despite the awful thing that had happened to Hannah Bradlow.

The police were still searching for the killer and luckily nobody had found out that Judith had been there at the scene. Thank goodness! She had pushed the experience down into a well-hidden compartment and didn't often think about it these days.

Life had to go on and Christmas was a crucial time in business when clients and suppliers had to be entertained. The company closed for the holidays only right before Christmas and nothing would fill the void for Judith of being at the little apartment for a few days all on her own – except the celebrations with her family, of course. And David was no longer part of her life. Judith wasn't looking forward to the holidays. She didn't like being alone and having too much time to think.

Another red ball flew past her head and Anthony Sedibe caught it with ease. He was one of the company's best fielders. Her boss, Mr. Ryker, was batting and none too happy when he had to hand over to the next batsman.

This whole action cricket thing was much harder than she'd anticipated, but Judith was not willing to let the fact that she had close to no experience stand in her way. She would do her best. She'd managed to get through worse. Much worse.

The MultoPharm team was playing in one of the outdoor pitches at the action cricket place. Nine pitches were separated from each other by strong nets anchored to the concrete ground. Like cages lined up next to each other.

It had only been two weeks since the incident in Killarney and David's inglorious departure from her life the following week. He hadn't phoned her since. He didn't have to. She knew he was still in South Africa and who had taken her place.

Judith was right, of course. It had been a breakup.

Charné, one of her friends from Pretoria had phoned to tell Judith the latest news about David. He had a new girlfriend, called Irma Boshoff. Apparently, they had all been to Hoër Meisieskool and Irma was just a year below their grade, but Judith couldn't remember her at all.

Charné said that Irma was blonde and busty. Unsurprisingly, Judith assumed that if David preferred this Irma to her, she must have something special, something she didn't have. Judith had looked her up on Facebook. Not very pretty, but definitely very different to herself. She'd phoned David and shouted at him. He apologised with some trivial excuse and hung up eventually only to phone her back a few days later to ask if he could still drop off his cat. Jealousy gripped her heart every time she thought of them together, but what could she do? She'd agreed to take the cat without question.

"Don't worry about them," Anthony Sedibe said in a fatherly tone. What was he talking about? "I don't know many girls who play cricket well."

Right... he was talking about cricket and not about David and Irma.

"Oh? What about Janet from Marketing? I thought she's a great fielder," Judith answered lightly. "She offered to give me lessons, but it's too late now, I suppose."

Another ball zoomed past her.

"That's crappy fielding!" A tall guy with a face that was redder than his hair yelled.

"Take it easy on her, man. She's a rookie. Don't you see that she's taking a break?" Andy turned back to her. "Are you ready to play again?"

"Yes thanks, Tony. I'll do my best."

Judith fastened the helmet strap under her chin and clapped her gloved hands together. She didn't manage to catch the next ball that flew in her direction, but the next two were not hit as hard by the batsman and she stretched and caught them both. Judith felt triumphant.

"Ah, we're getting the hang of it, are we?" Elizabeth, another accountant winked at her. Elizabeth was one of the two batsmen. Apart from Jane, she was the best female player on the MultoPharm team. She seemed suitably impressed and Judith gave Elizabeth a nod. Then she dropped the next ball.

"Darn!" Someone shouted and the team guffawed. There had been no hazing compared to KYMP, where she'd walked into the office one morning during the first week and her computer files had all been scrambled. A bit of guffawing at action cricket was nothing compared to the mean laughter she'd received before.

"I just need a bit more practice," Judith shouted back and did better as the allocated hour progressed.

In the end, they lost. It was only a practice match, but Judith felt as if she'd let everybody on her team down.

"Don't be so hard on yourself," Anthony said in the minibus when they were on the way back to the MultoPharm parking lot. "It will be better next year.

"Well, Tony. I guess it will. What's going on here?"

The minibus was turning into the broad driveway and stopped at the gate. Blue lights were flashing inside and police officers were standing by the entrance to the reception.

Judith's heart dropped.

"Hey Sandile, come here. What's up over there?" The red-haired guy, who was driving, asked the security guard and pointed to the flashing lights. The gate opened and the guard stepped up to the driver's window.

The man's hands were shaking as he spoke. "Something terrible has happened…" His mouth quivered.

"What is it? Spell it out!" The red-haired guy asked impatiently.

Everybody moved up to the driver's window to hear what the security guard had to say. The man shook his head in apparent horror.

"They found a dead body over there…" He pointed to a lawn with trees. It was at the far end of the grounds just by the fence that formed a decisive line on top of the slope to separate the highway from the MultoPharm parking lot. Below, the highway was still humming with traffic even at this time of day.

"Not another one," the driver of their minibus whispered. "What's going on around here? I mean this is Joburg, but we've never had something like this before."

First Hannah Bradlow was killed at her apartment in Killarney, then just three weeks ago a man had been found stabbed to death not two blocks from here, and now this! To everyone's mind, a vicious killer was still on the loose.

"Who was it?" Elizabeth wanted to know with tears in her eyes.

"John Bhengu."

"John, our receptionist?" Everyone moved back from the driver's window as if poison was entering the van. This couldn't possibly be true! Johan Bhengu was such a jovial and helpful young man, well-beloved by everyone in the company. Who would want to kill him?

"Yes, it's him. He was stabbed in the back." Tears ran down the security guard's face as he proceeded to wave the minibus into the parking lot.

Chapter THREE

Popcorn winced and jumped up and down on the backseat. The little white poodle didn't like car rides very much and always got hyper when it was time to go to the vet. Charlie and Jono tried to explain to him that there was nothing to worry about before each trip, but he didn't seem to believe them.

Billie, the beagle crossbreed, on the other hand, sat quietly on the backseat and looked astonished at the world flying past outside. She was doing her best to ignore the hyperactive Popcorn and only growled a little at a pedestrian, who dared to walk too closely to the car and stared at her through the back window.

Jono's cell phone played its usual tune and he switched off the classical music he had been playing to soothe the dogs. Charlie was trying to get hold of him.

"Sit down Popcorn!" Jono ordered and the little woolly pooch sat down on the floor in front of the backseat. Jono plugged the cell phone into the speaker system, so he could speak with his sister while driving.

Popcorn was trying to get through between the seats now, ready to jump onto the empty front seat. "Stay there, Popcorn," Jono scolded.

Charlie overheard the stern tone he used with Popcorn. 'What's going on? What is he doing?'

'Oh, nothing wild. Just the usual dance and I think he got a bit excited when he heard your voice. Sit down Poppie. There we go, good boy.' The little poodle jumped on the backseat and snuggled up to an unwilling Billie.

'Okay. Marius and his colleague Karen will be at the Piccachu Bar at about 6 o'clock. I don't want to be late. Can you make it home by five?'

'I will try. Why did I let you talk me into this? By the way… thank you dearest brother for taking the dogs to the vet for their injections…' Jono said in a joking tone.

'Ah, of course,' Charlie replied in the same tone. 'You know how much I appreciate it when you take them.'

'It's my pleasure sis, and luckily I'm done with my work for today. It's Friday and I'm kinda looking forward to our double-date. Hope the police lady is not a witch that turns me into a frog or arrests me or something.'

'I highly doubt it. According to Marius, she's turning heads at the headquarters.'

'Oh, I didn't know that. I'm more thinking of her personality.' Jono seemed a little nervous about the prospect of double-dating with a tough police inspector. Maybe he shouldn't watch all these clichéd murder stories on Netflix.

'Of course, you do. Lol. I guess we'll have to wait and see. If she starts bitching at you, we'll just have to think of a little white lie and leave.'

'Deal. My last date didn't go so well. Total nut case.'

'The IT lady? I know. Sorry, but she really seemed like a nice woman online.'

'Yeah, I know and then she only talked about her ex-boyfriend the whole time and how horrible her parents are - couldn't get a word in edgewise. I think I'm scarred for life.' Jono moaned.

'Or just for the next two weeks,' Charlie laughed. 'But you must admit that her dress-sense was kinda funny. Hello Kitty all the way. With a jungle twist.'

'You can say that again.'

Both of them chuckled. Jono had taken selfies with his date, in case Charlie didn't believe him. She was wearing a jungle-motif little dress with a dark Hello Kitty face on the front. The woman, whose name was Josie, had pressed herself against Jono and nuzzled his ear in one of the selfies. That had effectively ended the date, but it was difficult for Jono to live down the Me-Tarzan – You-Jane jokes.

'Your face was priceless, especially in that last selfie. How did the dogs behave at the vet?' Charlie asked her brother.

'They were good little fur babies. Popcorn flirted with the vet's assistant from the word go. I swear he was smiling at her.'

'That little Casanova.' Charlie laughed with a sense of maternal pride. 'So no more crying and peeing while you were there?'

Jono pulled off as the traffic light turned green and Popcorn was getting restless again.

'Just for a couple of minutes or so. Then they behaved themselves all the way. Dr. Cooper was really nice, too. Popcorn's just a little overexcited now. Get back Poppie!' Jono tried to close the gap between the seats with his arm. 'Billie is taking everything in her stride. I'm quite proud of her.'

'Are you coping there?'

'Yeah, he's just trying to join me in the front and I can't drive with a poodle sitting on my lap.'

'Should be a chick-magnet,' Charlie joked.

'Thanks, sis. I'm a chick-magnet even without a poodle. Get back. Sit down.' Jono was sharing his attention between his sister and the little dog.

'No doubt. At least they've got their shots for another year. Did you ask the vet what can be done about the awful neighbour's dogs?'

'I did. Dr. Cooper said that we are not the only ones complaining about people not putting their dogs on leashes when they walk them in the street. I better don't tell you what he called them, but apart from going to the police, there's not much you can do. A dachshund came in only yesterday with a bite wound to the nose that needed stitches. Only that's when the SPCA intervenes. Damn.'

Jono turned left and had to stop for a rubbish collector to wheel bins to the side of the road. Finally, he was able to overtake the truck.

'Really, I thought you could report negligent dog owners. Poor thing…'

'I know. Apparently, it's not that straightforward. Lucky that Billie didn't need stitches. Putting that antiseptic cream on was just the right thing to do. Vet says we should film the dogs when they are outside without a leash and post it online. We can also do an affidavit at the police station… hang on… I'll phone you right back.'

A lone policeman was waving him down and Jono instantly thought that he should have slowed the car down instead of speeding up when he was overtaking the rubbish truck. He'd seen a camera flashing at the car in front of him, but he hadn't been speeding. He pressed a button to switch off the phone connection and pulled into a parking bay on the side of the road.

Jono rolled down the window and gave the policeman a big smile. The two dogs on the back seat started barking when the police officer started talking. He told Jono that he'd been driving too fast.

"I'm sorry, officer, how fast did I drive?"

"You were going 63 km and it's a 60 km zone."

The police officer checked if the license stuck to the windscreen was valid. It was. Jono tried to think of a way to quickly get out of the situation. Charlie was waiting at home.

"I'm really sorry, officer. See, I'm taking the dogs home from the vet. They got their injections today and…"

"Can I see your driver's licence?" The policeman interrupted him rudely.

Jono handed the man his International licence. American. Bloody foreigners, the police officer thought. Perfect. They usually didn't put up a fight.

"I'll have to write you a ticket, sir." He took out a notepad and wrote something down that Jono couldn't read.

"Is that really necessary? I was only 3 km over the speed limit," Jono objected.

"Sir, you were breaking the law. Maybe in your country, it's different, but here we are strict, you see. I think that's a good enough problem."

This was not the first conversation with a motorist the police officer was having today.

"I understand, officer, is there nothing you can do?

You see - the dogs…"

Billie and Popcorn obviously didn't like the intrusion by the arm-of-the-law very much. They growled at the policeman and he glared at them.

"Tell your dogs to be quiet," The policeman demanded and the dogs barked even louder.

"I can't, officer, they are a little upset. I'm trying to tell you… they've just been to the vet…"

"We have a problem, sir…"

"So what are we going to do about the problem?" Jono was not yet familiar with the ways of Johannesburg's traffic police, although he'd heard stories of officers wanting to supplement their income just before weekends.

"You are lucky that I'm in a good mood today," the policeman said. "If you help me out, I'm going to help you out."

Jono grasped where this was going. The weekend was around the corner and cars were randomly stopped for minor transgressions. At least that's what he'd heard. It was the first time he'd ever been stopped, but friends of his had had unpleasant experiences. Maybe because they were driving better cars.

"How much are we talking?" Jono wanted to know. The dogs were calming down.

"How much do you have with you?" The policeman drew his face into an oily grin.

"I think I have maybe 180 or 200 Rand."

"Make it 250."

Jono didn't have much time to discuss the matter or haggle the price down. Charlie was waiting at home and she wouldn't be pleased if they were late for her first date with Marius Vorster. She seemed to like the inspector. So he decided to go along with the man's demand.

"Alright, let me see. Shush, Billie, Popcorn!" The dogs stopped barking and started growling again when the officer moved too fast for their liking. Jono bent down and checked his wallet in the glove compartment, while the policeman got into position, placing his elbow on the open window.

It wasn't hard to read how this would go down.

"Here we go. One hundred… two hundred… and fifty." Jono stuck the folded banknotes between the policeman's elbow and his chest.

"What about the other twenty Rand in your purse?"

Jono knew that this was not the time to put the policeman right on the difference between a wallet and a purse, but he was surprised that the man had spotted the twenty Rand.

"I need a little bit of cash on me. See, my sister is going out with this police inspector tonight. Actually, two police inspectors. It's a double-date. What was your name again?"

The officer quickly picked up the notes and said, "never mind, sir, have a good evening." As he moved, his name badge became visible.

"Officer Mdluli... I'm sure to give Inspector Vorster your best."

"Am I supposed to know some Inspector Vorster?" Officer Mdluli barked at him.

"He's working in Homicide. In fact, why don't we call him right now to say hello? I'm sure he'll understand why he must wait for my sister and me to arrive. You can explain it to him."

He picked up his cell phone and pressed a few buttons.

"Bah..." The traffic policeman snorted. He didn't seem quite so smug anymore and threw the notes through the open window at Jono.

His quick movements startled the dogs and they began to bark again.

"Thank you, officer Mdluli. That's very big of you." Jono grinned and started the engine. That could have just as easily backfired, but it seemed that he was off the hook for now.

The policeman didn't listen. He walked away, already waving down another car, ready to fleece the driver. Jono didn't wait for him to change his mind. He'd been lucky this time. "Okay, okay guys, just be quiet now," he calmed down the dogs and made a quick escape as soon as he saw a gap, driving in traffic that got heavier by the minute. He was already running late now and by the time, he got home, it was half-past five.

"Where have you been?" Charlie didn't seem impressed with her brother anymore. She had changed into a cute feminine top and skinny jeans and had put on some makeup. *Charlie always looks great with makeup on*, Jono thought. If this Marius-guy didn't see that then he must be blind.

"I already fed the dogs." Charlie seemed a little

nervous. Ah, she liked the guy!

"Sorry, I was stopped by the traffic police. 3 km over the limit of 60." Jono drove up the driveway and Charlie opened the back door of the car. The two pooches jumped out and up Charlie's legs.

"Okay, okay… what 3 kilometres? That's not even speeding."

"I know, but what was I supposed to do. I was busy handing over all my cash when he changed his mind and threw the money back at me."

"Why did he do that?" Charlie asked.

"I guess he didn't like the idea of saying hello to a couple of police inspectors." Jono grinned.

"You didn't…"

"Oh, but I did. Can I change now, please? I don't want to bowl over the inspector-lady with pungent dog-smell. There won't be time for a shower."

"Sure not. We have to go just now."

Jono just had time to change his trousers and put a clean shirt on. Charlie was already waiting in the car.

"I put the dogs in the kitchen. Even turned on the radio. Classical music keeps them calm."

"Great, let's go!"

It was hot so close to Christmas and it was even hotter in the car even this late. Ten minutes later, they arrived at the Piccachu restaurant and had to circle the parking lot for a few minutes. Marius Vorster was already waiting at a table by the window with a glass of Coca Cola and a water jug in front of him.

He had chosen the table well. The view of the treed suburb from here all the way to Midrand was magnificent.

"I'm so sorry, Marius," Charlie apologised. "Jono drove too fast and…"

They sat down and poured themselves some water before ordering drinks.

"I was driving only 63 km in a 60 km zone and. I had the dogs in the car with me. He stopped me and wanted money…" Jono explained.

"Wow, slowly… I've only been waiting here for ten minutes. That's no train smash in South Africa, you know... Karen is not even here yet. What were you saying about being stopped?"

Jono gulped down a glass of water before answering.

"This police officer stopped me in Norwood and wanted me to bribe him," Jono continued his story.

"250 Rand. That was just about everything I had in my wallet. I've heard about this sort of thing, but it was the first time it happened to me."

"Dang! What did you do?" Marius Vorster asked.

Charlie ordered a Coke zero for herself and a glass of red wine for Jono. She was the designated driver for after their night out and wouldn't touch alcohol.

"I told him about you." Jono scoffed. "And he threw the money back in my face."

"There's no way, a traffic cop would know inspectors in Homicide."

"Well, it worked. Maybe he's not as experienced yet…"

"Do you have the officer's name? Asking for a bribe is a serious offence for an officer of the law. And we're coming down on corruption, at last."

"His name's Mdluli. It's almost the weekend and time to earn himself a little bonus, I guess. I heard that's pretty common."

"That's no excuse for such behaviour. There's been too much of that sort of thing going on. Some drivers complain to IPID, the Independent Police Investigative Directorate, about these incidents. Even in Homicide, rich people try to bribe their way out of a tight spot. Dockets disappearing or escaping from courtrooms. It just shows that there's been a market for it."

"Why am I not surprised? Jono stated.

"Well, they are having a difficult time now. Ever since the new Police Commissioner took over. He's trying to get rid of those bad apples."

"Glad to hear it."

"Yes, it's about time. I've heard that foreigners are being targeted now in the affluent areas. They are intimidated and even threatened. I'm ashamed of those officers in the force. Sometimes, the cops are real and sometimes they are not. Perhaps we can turn things around one little incident at a time."

"So what must a driver do, foreign or not, if a police officer asked for a bribe?" Jono asked and Marius handed Jono a business card.

"Phone this number and speak to Colonel Botha. He's a good friend and will do something about this Officer Mdluli, I can promise you that. As to everybody else, all I can think of is that they should get names and license numbers and report the problem to IPID."

"Alright, I'll spread the word. Can you put that into your bag?" Jono asked Charlie and gave her his wallet. "This place is great. Just look at that view!"

"I love this venue," Charlie said dreamily and took a sip of her coke. "We don't come to Sandton often."

"I'm glad you like it," Marius Vorster said with a smile. "Place opened only last month."

"Stunning." Charlie got up and stood close to the railing that was topped with a row of flower pots. "The view is so clear since it rained last week." She admired the sunset that spread a golden light over the suburb before disappearing below the horizon. The waitress handed out the oversized menus.

"Yes, it does make a difference," Inspector Vorster said. "Let's wait with ordering until Karen comes. She sent me a message just now that she's delayed."

Marius seemed a little nervy around Charlie and Jono noticed it with satisfaction. He definitely liked his sister!

They chatted and ordered more water with lemon. After another fifteen minutes, a wiry woman of about forty with short blonde hair strode confidently toward their table. She was dressed in jeans and a simple beige t-shirt and wore no makeup. Jono thought she was quite attractive nevertheless.

"Hi, I'm Karen van der Merwe," she introduced herself to Charlie and Jono with a firm handshake. The woman spoke with an Afrikaans accent. She was originally from Pretoria and had been transferred to Johannesburg only recently. Johannesburg was only an hour's drive away from the country's capital.

"Nice to meet you, Karen. I'm Charlie and this is my brother Jono."

"Really? That's different." She was no doubt alluding to Charlie being white and Jono being Asian. "Nice to meet you. So you are my date for tonight?" She said in a firm tone and ogled Jono. He coughed a little and pulled his hand back. Charlie giggled a little. Maybe Jono thought she was a witch for real.

"I am the very same," he confirmed. "Nice to meet you, Karen. We hear that you started working at Homicide downtown only this month."

"Yes, I did. It's almost three weeks now," the blonde woman answered.

The waitress came to their table to take orders, but

Karen wasn't ready yet.

"How do you like it there?" Charlie asked politely, while the waiter put a menu in front of the female inspector. Karen took the menu and held it up as if to shield herself from her unwanted date and addressed Charlie, who sat next to her.

"Well, it's still early days and there's a lot of work to do." She looked at Jono briefly from behind the menu before giving Marius a lingering look that didn't lack tenderness.

"A bit more going on than in Sunnyside, where I worked before. Things are shaping up, though. Great colleagues." The remark was clearly aimed at her new colleague Marius Vorster. He cleared his voice.

"Hmmm… thank you, I guess," Marius said and didn't know where to look.

Charlie was surprised at the woman's demeanour. Marius had told her that they had barely exchanged pleasantries so far and apart from meeting at obligatory briefings with the whole team, they'd barely had direct contact. No mention of a possible crush on her good-looking colleague.

Marius didn't seem to catch the vibe. He'd told

Charlie that he wanted to invite Karen to the double date because she'd made it clear that there wasn't much going on in her social life and that she would like to see more of Johannesburg. Maybe he wasn't sure whether Charlie liked him, so a double-date had seemed like a good solution to make her feel more comfortable.

Karen van der Merwe had transferred to Johannesburg to be close to her elderly parents at an old age home in Westcliff. He knew that she was hard-working and kept her head down. No man in her life. That was basically it.

He paid attention to the menu again.

"Would you like to order a drink before we order the food?" Marius asked her and Karen answered a little too quickly.

"Sure. Same as you." That was odd.

"It's just Coke," he said.

"In that case, can I have white wine, please? If Marius gives me a lift home, I can let my hair down a bit." She looked at Jono and Charlie with a big grin on her face. "Always appreciate a dedicated driver."

"Yes, Charlie and I have the same arrangement. I

get to drink tonight," Jono said.

"Alright then." Marius held up his hand and the waitress rushed over to take the order. "Could you bring us a white wine, please?"

"Would you also like to order the food, sir?"

"Sure, I'm having the steak with green peppercorn sauce and chips…" he began.

They all knew what they wanted to eat, but Karen took a couple of minutes to study the menu and asked Marius for his opinion. After a patient wait, the waiter repeated each order and walked to the bar. The white wine arrived before the food and now the conversation began to flow more easily. Mostly between the two police inspectors.

"He didn't say that…" Karen van der Merwe laughed.

"Yes, he did." Marius Vorster still seemed oblivious to how his new colleague gave him sideways looks.

"Said what?" Charlie wanted to know. This insider conversation became boring. "Don't you want to let us in on the joke?"

Marius explained what had been said by a drug

dealer they'd arrested for murdering one of his runners, but for the life of her, Charlie couldn't find anything funny about it. She changed the subject and asked Marius about his last Christmas vacation. He had taken his daughter to Sun City so that his ex-wife could go away to the coast with her new boyfriend. That boyfriend was no longer in the picture, so this year plans would be different.

That's interesting, Charlie thought.

The restaurant seemed to reach capacity as more and more people without reservations entered. Most of them were settled at the bar and a long narrow table by the railing, looking out into the balmy night.

Halfway through their meal, Karen began to make snippy remarks about Charlie's looks.

Especially her different eye colours and the flowy top she was wearing.

"I can't stand ruffles," she scoffed at the mere thought. "Way too fussy for me."

"Oh well, everybody is different," Marius Vorster replied in his date's defence. "I quite like flowy tops on women. That green colour suits you very well, Charlie."

"Why thank you, good sir," Charlie said with a forgiving smile. "I'm glad you like it."

"I have a dress with flounces," Karen said quickly and smiled at Marius. "Bought it ages ago. Maybe when we go dancing one of these days, I'll wear it."

Marius still didn't seem to notice how eager she was to get his attention, but then men often didn't pick up on little details like that. He cut off a piece of his steak and seemed quite happy with his food.

Charlie, on the other hand, began to get irritated with Karen. "I can't really imagine a woman arresting drug dealers in flouncy dresses," she said and winked at her.

"Neither can I," the female inspector laughed. The women seemed to have reached an impasse as far as their wardrobes were concerned. Jono noticed the slight tension between them and decided to intervene.

"Swell. How's your fish?" He asked Karen, trying to be a good date.

"It's lovely. Moist and tasty. Fish can be so dry, especially at restaurants. Tried to eat vegan for a while, but it's not for me," she replied.

"Oh, you're in luck then. This is a very good

restaurant. Fish is one of their specialities," Charlie said and smiled sweetly. "Vegan's not that easy to find, even in Joburg."

"Whatever you say." Karen gave a little laugh and started to work on her Basa with garlic and lemon sauce again.

Charlie was taken aback by the brusque reaction and decided to draw back a little. Why would she want to battle over a man's attention anyway? They barely knew each other and if this was how it's going to be, good luck to them.

"Many of my Pretoria friends think that fish is salad, Chicken a vegetable and meat's proper food," Marius said and they all laughed.

"That's true," Karen agreed and gave him a bright smile. "In Pretoria meat's the order of the day. And men just love to braai. But all that meat can cause health problems. My brother-in-law has high blood pressure and high cholesterol and he's not the only one in the family. That's why I thought that vegan would be better, but I'm fine without red meat."

"Hey, my steak suddenly doesn't taste that nice anymore," Marius joked.

"Mine is still as delicious as the first bite," Jono said and held up his knife as if to make his point.

"How's your chicken – sorry, vegetables – Charlie?" Marius asked.

"Great. Really good," Charlie said and enjoyed the look in Marius' eyes even more than his thoughtful question.

Despite the initially unpleasant undertones, they were whiling away the evening pleasantly enough and called it a night at 9 o'clock. Karen was a little drunk and Marius gave her a lift home as promised. They had parked at opposite ends of the carpark and said goodnight at the entrance to the restaurant.

"If I didn't know better, I'd say that our blonde policewoman is a little bit jealous of you," Jono declared as they were in the car on their way home.

"Maybe we should give her the benefit of the doubt. She might just be insecure, being new in town and not knowing us," Charlie said good-naturedly. She never held onto a grudge for long. "She's more familiar with Marius than us."

"Yeah, whatever you say, sis," Jono grinned and Charlie cuffed her brother on the arm while turning at a traffic light. "They don't seem to know each other very well."

"Hey, don't get me wrong, she irritated me in the beginning when she became snarky with me. Then I imagined her in a romantic flouncy dress doing karate or something and I found that funny."

"Really?" Jono asked with a grin.

"Yes really. She's feisty, but I don't think she's malicious. Marius didn't seem to think anything of it."

"Duh, so she's feisty. Not unusual for a policewoman. So how did you like going out with your inspector for once?"

"He's not MY inspector… and I thought he was really nice. A true gentleman. Can you believe that his Dad owns a wine farm in Stellenbosch?"

"Yeah, what's he doing here in Joburg, then?" Jono yawned and leaned back in his seat. "I mean he could have a cushy life in Stellenbosch and instead he fights crime here in the South African crime capital."

"I think it's because of his daughter. He's divorced and his daughter is a teenager. He probably wants to be involved in her life," Charlie said. "His ex-wife moved to Joburg to be with her boyfriend, who's now her ex, and took the daughter with her."

"Hmm, speaks for his character. A lot of men run for the hills after a divorce."

"Yes, they do. At least, that's what I've been told," Charlie answered.

"So, any butterflies yet?" Jono chuckled. He was a little tipsy.

"What butterflies?" Charlie asked with an innocent look. "We are just working on cases together. Sometimes. And he's a nice guy. That's all."

"You can't tell ME that. I know you better than that. How many men have you had a date with recently?"

"It wasn't a date as such. We just went out together over a meal and to get to know each other a little better. And in any case, you saw how things are developing between the two of them, so what's the big deal?"

"It's no big deal and I'm glad that you come out of your shell a bit. You should consider going on another date with the good detective. Only the two of you…"

"If he asks me, I might consider it." Charlie overtook a slow car.

Jono shrugged and closed his eyes a little. When they turned into their street, one of the houses was brightly lit. The neighbours with the aggressive dogs were standing in the street with a number of visitors, having a chat and a laugh. Music was thudding in the background before somebody turned it down. It wasn't the first time that a party at that neighbour's place continued outside for a while longer. The pleasant neighbours around them stoically bore the noise.

"Oh my." Jono sat up in his seat, annoyance in his voice. "Do these people know the difference between private and public space?"

"Doesn't seem like it." Charlie scoffed. She'd spotted the two large dogs among the guests. They had attacked Billie through their gate. "I prefer to ignore them. Did we forget to switch on the lights when we left?"

"Wait, I think we're having a power failure." The music and bright lights in the street had gone off for good, so a power failure was the most likely explanation. They heard Popcorn and Billie wincing inside the dark kitchen. Charlie drew up into the driveway and jumped out to close the gate. The last thing they needed was the neighbours' dogs run onto the property now.

"Sorry, babies," Jono called through the kitchen gate in an upbeat tone. "We're back. All is good."

The dogs were scratching at the door, but Charlie couldn't find the key.

"It's so dark, I can't see anything…"

Jono held up his cell phone torchlight.

"Thanks. Okay, got it," she sighed. "Where are the candles?"

As they walked into the dark kitchen and patted the excited pair of pooches, Charlie's cell phone rang. Lerato's name lit up on the screen.

"It's Lerato," she said to Jono. He nodded and Charlie answered her phone, while her brother lit a couple of candles in the kitchen with matches and switched on the kettle. He then walked through the house to light the remaining candles.

They knew the drill when it came to the frequent power outages.

In the darkness, the Christmas decoration had been invisible, but now, the green and red and gold of the wreath on the kitchen door, the pine and lit candles spread festive cheer in the kitchen. The rest of the house didn't look any different and soon they would be decorating the artificial tree with straw stars and tinsel, which Charlie had bought on special this week.

'Sorry to bother you so late. How was your date with Marius?' Lerato asked.

'Can't you wait until tomorrow morning to find out? We just got home.' Charlie placed the candles in the kitchen in different places and searched for the dog treats on the shelf behind the door.

'That's not why I'm phoning.' Lerato sounded serious.

'Then why are you phoning?' Charlie asked her. She'd found the treats and the dogs waited for them sitting down patiently.

'We have a murder case on our hands…' Lerato said.

'A murder case? Why is that so urgent that you have to phone me in the middle of the night?' Charlie gave the dogs their treats.

'It's just sometimes like that. If you work a case, you must be prepared to go out at night. I need you to scan the place for something that could help us.'

'Alright, I get it.' Charlie put away the treats and the

pooches begged for more. "No, you guys that's it."

'What?'

'I'm talking to the dogs, not you," Charlie explained.

'Oh okay… Johan called me to come to the scene just now and I thought can pick you up. Perhaps we'll find something important while the iron is hot, so to speak.'

'Wait, what?' The last thing Charlie felt like doing was look at a dead body after a pleasant evening out.

'It's not too late, is it? I can pop around in five minutes or seven if I drive more civilised. See you then.' Click. Lerato had hung up and it was too late to object.

"What did she want?" Jono asked as he came back into the kitchen.

He sat down at the kitchen table and one dog jumped on his lap, while the other one tried to jump up as well. The kettle was already boiling. Jono got up to make tea and the dogs followed him. Charlie exhaled deeply and put her phone on the counter.

"No rest for the wicked, it seems. Lerato said she needs to go out to a murder scene. Actually, she wants me to come with her to look at a dead body in case I can pick something up. She'll be here just now. Should I change?"

She looked down at herself, at the flouncy top and dark jeans and low heels.

"I think don't stress about clothes, unless the crime scene is in muddy terrain. Then I'd put some other shoes on."

"She didn't say where it was."

Jono handed his sister a cup of tea. "Here, let's sit down for a bit and switch gear before she comes." The respite didn't last very long. Soon, a car hooted outside.

"That must be Lerato," Charlie sighed and grabbed her phone and handbag.

"Yeah, or it's another one of the neighbours' party guests," Jono sneered.

Charlie looked out the window and saw the faint outline of Lerato's car in front of their gate. "I know, but it's Lerato, alright. I better get going before she hoots again. Sorry, you'll have to drink tea without me. See you later. Bye, babies."

She put on lip balm and closed the kitchen gate behind her.

"Yup… I'll probably be asleep when you get back," Jono grumbled.

"I'll be fine. See you in the morning, then. Bye!"

Charlie walked carefully down the driveway and greeted her friend. Lerato leaned over to open the passenger door for her.

"Hey doll. What are all those people doing in your dark road?"

"They were having a party and they don't seem to mind the power failure," Charlie explained and got into the passenger seat.

"Ah well, that's strange."

"They are strange neighbours."

"Street lights in the area aren't all off. Hyde Park seems to have power. Let's hope that we won't be driving all the way in the dark."

"Well, we'll see."

"Thanks for coming with me, Charlie. Crime scene's at a company in Marlboro." They drove down the dark street with not even the moon to light their way.

Chapter FOUR

Lerato answered Charlie's questions about the murder case on the way to the crime scene. At least what Johan had told her so far.

"So, who is our hapless victim?" Charlie tried to slot into PI mode as difficult as it was.

"Victim is male and worked for the pharmaceutical company, where he was found. In the parking lot by the highway. Apparently, it was the receptionist."

"The receptionist? A robbery? But why were we called in?" Charlie probed.

"No, Johan said it wasn't a robbery. At least, nothing was taken. From the MO, it may have been an inside job."

"An inside job? Why the receptionist? What's the name of the company?"

"Don't know yet and it's Multo… something. The vic had been working at the reception for about three years."

"The MultoPharm Corporation?" Charlie kept

peppering questions at Lerato.

"Yes, I think that's the name of the company. How do you know?"

"Just a guess. I went there for an interview last year," Charlie explained. "It's an international company, so I thought I might have a chance."

"Didn't work out, I suppose?" Lerato switched gears and they drove faster.

"No, it didn't. Nice place, though. I remember the willow trees in the garden. There were park benches for the employees and even a pond with ducks."

"Really? Sounds like they care about their staff."

"Well, the manager I met was all keen as mustard. Said that he wanted me to come in for a second interview, but then I never heard back from him. It was probably best that things didn't work out with them."

"That's pretty shitty. Sorry," Lerato said.

There were barely any people out in the streets, they negotiated, but the streetlights were on and the traffic lights were working.

"Oh, that's alright," Charlie answered. "Working with you isn't so bad either, you know. I heard on the news that there was some internal problem at MultoPharm. Dodgy bookkeeping, or something. It even made the news."

"Well, good riddance then. Perhaps the court case has something to do with the murder… I wouldn't be surprised."

"But the receptionist?" Charlie held on to the door as Lerato turned into a dark street. This area seemed to have a power failure as well. These outages were becoming more frequent of late and were making life in a city like Johannesburg more difficult.

"Thank goodness, the GPS is still working," Lerato said relieved.

At the roundabout, take the first exit…

"Thank goodness. I'm not sure I could find the company again in the dark."

"No need for that." Lerato turned at the dark traffic lights slowly into the main road. She went on to tell Charlie how the man had died - by stabbing - and the circumstances of how the body had been detected by his colleagues earlier.

"It's not so bad working with you, you know," Charlie said.

"I should think so," Lerato laughed.

Charlie yawned.

"Tired?" Lerato asked her, "or am I just boring you?"

"Just a bit tired. Making small talk with the new inspector, Karen van der Merwe, was awkward. She seems to have a crush on Marius and got a bit snarky with me. But the food was good and the view was even better."

"Wait, what? I thought you had a double date with Jono. Wasn't he supposed to take her off your hands so you and Marius can talk?" Lerato didn't take her eyes off the road.

"He tried and she seemed to like the attention - mostly, but she was a little intimidating even for him. And she liked talking to Marius better."

"Really? Why do you think that is?"

"Who knows?"

"Probably just the police vibe… oh I know. You think she has a thing for Marius, right?"

Charlie yawned again. "Maybe. Jono thinks that Marius likes me. We didn't get a chance to talk about him, because you phoned just after we got home."

"Yeah, blame it on me." Lerato grinned. "Are you going on another date with Marius, then? Just the two of you?" Lerato was now the one, who asked all the questions. *Keep to your left, turn slightly to the left…*

Lerato turned left, then went under a bridge then took a sharp right.

"Jono said the same thing. Actually, I don't feel like dating anyway. If he asks me, I'll go." Charlie shrugged. "Otherwise, we'll see each other again when we work on some other murder case."

"Not tonight, because he's off duty."

"Good."

"Gosh, You can be so old-fashioned," Lerato rolled her eyes.

"Why not? I'm just like that." Charlie countered. "You asked Peter out, didn't you?"

"Nooo, I just nudged him a bit." Lerato winked at her friend.

"Yeah right." Charlie grew serious. "To be honest, I don't know what I'm thinking. It's been three years since Colin… since the accident. Maybe it's too soon. What if I like Marius? He's a policeman, that's a dangerous job. I couldn't go through something like that again. Losing someone, I mean."

"Don't worry too much about it, Charlie. Don't rush things if you feel it's too soon. If it's meant to be, it will be."

"Wise old lady…"

"Hey, watch it, young lady," Lerato chuckled.

In 400 meters, carry on straight… you have reached your destination on the right. The automated GPS voice directed them through the last stretch of the way.

"Oh look, we are here. It must be over there." They turned into the entrance to the parking lot, but the large gate was closed. Lerato hooted a couple of times. The area was pitch dark, but the lights were on at MultoPharm.

"They must have a generator. Actually, it's pretty likely for a company."

Charlie recognised the location. "I was definitely here for the interview," she said.

Lerato hooted again and the large gate opened and she drove in to park the car. Inspector Johan Phaladi was talking to CSI technicians not far away. As he caught sight of the two PIs, he took his protective silicon gloves off and came to meet them. He knew who they were, of course. This wasn't the first case they'd collaborated on.

"Is he the only one on duty tonight?" Charlie asked.

"Yup, looks like it."

"Hi, thanks for coming," the police inspector greeted the two friends.

"Hi Johan, so what's the skinny on the situation?" Lerato inquired without much ado. "Victim still here?"

"Yes, over there," he answered and pointed to a treed area straight ahead. "Similarities to the murdered woman in Killarney last month," Inspector Phaladi answered in the same matter-of-fact tone. "Sort of. The Barler case… no, Bradlow. Hannah Bradlow." He read from his notes. "Worked at the same company."

They looked at him askance. "Also worked here? That can't be a coincidence. So what are the chances that the murders are linked? I didn't follow the case."

Her company, the Maitirelo Agency had not been involved in the investigations into the Barlow case, so she hadn't paid much attention to it and didn't recall the details. The inspector explained while paging back to his notes.

"Could be linked. We don't know yet. Bradlow was also stabbed in the back with a knife, but on top of it, she was pushed through an open ceiling-to-floor window and over the balcony. In her own apartment on the third floor. We found hardly any blood in the apartment, so she was pushed out into the backyard quickly after the stabbing."

"Or she fell?" Lerato offered.

"Unlikely. Probably didn't scream. No witnesses at the block of apartments where she lived and virtually no evidence left behind by the killer. Used victim's own kitchen knife. She ended up in the backyard with broken bones, but it was the knife wound that caused her death. Straight into the heart. She bled out in a half-sitting position."

"So she didn't scream?" Lerato asked.

"Neighbours didn't hear any screaming or the impact. But then there was this celebrity dance show on that night. It matches with the time of death. Everybody we spoke to was watching it. A maid found her in the morning when she carried a washing basket out to the back yard."

"So she'd been murdered the night before and laid there all night dead in the back and nobody noticed?" Lerato confirmed the facts.

"Yes, that's what the coroner said. As if being stabbed isn't bad enough. She was killed twice, so to speak." The inspector closed his notebook.

"Two stabbings now? Was our victim tonight also thrown off a balcony?"

"Not a balcony, but pushed down from higher ground. You see?" He turned around and pointed to the location, where a body was lying under a blanket. The traffic lower down behind a palisade fence roared even at this time of the night. The lights along the highway were thankfully not affected by the power outage. Their glare was in stark contrast to the virtual darkness around the highway.

Lerato pointed to the group of CSI technicians and the covered body on the ground. "Are they done yet?"

"Almost." Actually, he was pushed from up there. We found bloodstains." He pointed to a row of parking bays higher up. "Maybe to make sure he was dead."

"What? Perhaps, the killer tried to push him into

the traffic on the highway."

They scrutinised the location. A row of shrubs was blocking the view of the highway. Perhaps that's what blocked John Bhengu's fall. "If the man screamed at all, the traffic noise must have blocked it out. Again, nobody heard a thing," Inspector Phaladi said. "Come, have a look at the body."

He led the way as they started walking toward the murder scene.

"Weird. So, not exactly the same MO, then?" Charlie stated.

"No, not exactly," the inspector turned around to face her. "But two employees of the same company are murdered only weeks apart. Come on, what are the odds?"

He led the way past the brightly lit main entrance on the right to the obscure crime scene that was lit only by the lights along the highway.

"Name is John Bhengu."

"Yes, you said." Lerato tried to get a better look. She had seen worse crime scenes. "What else did you find out about him?"

"He's thirty four, married with two kids. I already

mentioned that he was a receptionist. Well liked, apparently. It was pretty hot today, so the time of death is unclear, but his shift ended at 4 o'clock this afternoon. He hung around for some assertiveness class he took with two other colleagues."

"That's impressive for a receptionist. Wanted to better himself."

"Part of their staff programme, I was told. The head of the legal department organised the training. That's the last time he was seen alive. A security guard found him just before a minibus with about six or seven employees arrived back from some action cricket training. They have a friendly tournament going with other companies."

"Have you searched the premises?" Lerato wanted to know.

"Just a superficial search. We're short-staffed tonight and the power outage isn't helping," the inspector said.

The road on the parking lot led up a slope, then around the building and back onto the main driveway. The killer could be hiding anywhere on the park-like grounds. Although a high palisade fence secured the perimeter toward the highway below, he could have found a way onto the property from that side.

"Hmm, they have no proper lighting here and the highway must have been roaring with rush-hour traffic earlier. No wonder that the victim wasn't detected sooner." Lerato studied the scene.

"What's the time of death?" She asked

"We don't know yet, possibly four to five hours ago."

"You think it might be a serial killer, then?" Charlie asked. "Someone, who has a grudge against this company?"

"Hard to say," Johan Phaladi answered. "Maybe, but two bodies don't make a serial killer yet. We just noticed the similar way the victims were murdered."

"And that they both worked for MultoPharm. Any suspects? Male perhaps?" Lerato asked. "Considering the brutality of the killings?"

"Not yet, we've spoken to the security guards on duty. They are still shaking. John Bhengu was a good guy, they assure me. Family man."

"Well, that doesn't mean much, but could rule them out."

Charlie counted her blessings that the job she'd

interviewed for hadn't materialised. "So what do you know so far?"

"During the investigations, none of Ms Bradlow's colleagues stood out. She worked in the Accounts Department."

"We have to speak to the staff members, who returned from action cricket."

"We'll arrange it," the inspector said.

They'd reached the prostrate body of the victim and stood by his head. Charlie hung back a little to look around by herself. She was not in the mood to see a dead body just now, after the fairly pleasant evening she'd had.

It wasn't unusual for her to try and get another angle of the situation, so Lerato let her be. Maybe Charlie could see something - or someone - that the others, herself included, could not.

"A receptionist and an accountant. Maybe the receptionist saw something he shouldn't have and was silenced," Lerato suggested. "Or maybe it was personal. A disgruntled ex-boyfriend… or worse, a jealous wife? Our perp here could even be a copycat."

The cover was down to the victim's shoulders. A

good-looking young man lay on his side as if he was sleeping. What a tragic end at the age of thirty four.

"Anything's possible at this stage. As I said, we haven't made much headway with the Bradlow case yet. Killer was careful not to leave evidence. Smudged bloodstains, that's all. No usable fingerprints or shoe prints. And as I said, neighbours didn't hear anything."

"Nothing? Oh yes, Strictly Come Dancing was on last night. Damn coincidence."

"Unless it was a planned hit. Then again, it was too amateurish for a hit and why an accountant and a receptionist? Nothing adds up. I suppose that's why they roped the Maitirelo Agency in this time." The inspector shrugged his shoulders.

"Is it likely that the killer drove onto the premises?"

"We're busy checking for any strange cars. Or he climbed over the fence from the highway's side. It's not a very high fence."

"Possibly, but look at those spikes. What else do we know?" Lerato wanted to know.

"As I said, the security guard found him. Then a minibus with our cricketers arrived back here. They are waiting over there." He pointed to the entrance where a group of people stood forlorn underneath the bright lights, too timid to move elsewhere.

"Right. We'll do our best to support you guys," Lerato said with confidence. "I'll need to see the case file and any evidence you have. If there's something to be found, we'll find it, I'm sure." She examined the stab wound of the victim, but the murder weapon was nowhere to be found.

"Murder weapon's missing. The wound's located pretty much in the same place as Ms Bradlow's stab wound." The inspector checked his notes. "Yep."

"Can the coroner give us a profile of the approximate height of the killer?"

"I'm sure he can," he answered. "Not too tall, I guess."

"Hmm. We should also speak to the neighbours again," Lerato continued. "I mean nobody heard anything when a woman is murdered and thrown off her third-storey apartment? That can't be. There must be something."

"In the Bradlow case, we thought that everything points to a work connection, but the case ran cold there." Johan Phaladi scratched his head.

"Or it could be both." Charlie pondered as she joined them next to the body. Poor man, she thought and tried not to look too closely. She had expected to see a bright speck or something to indicate that the victim was still around, watching the proceedings. But there was nothing at all. "Sounds like an insider job to me. You need a pass to get in…"

"Surveillance cameras?" Lerato addressed the inspector.

"Yes. Your guess is as good as mine," he said. "As I said we're still checking the footage. I'm thinking of bringing in a polygrapher this time. A polygraph test should clear up a few things."

"Yes, sounds good. Let's go to the action cricket players?" Lerato looked straight at him and got up. She had seen enough and one of the CSI technicians spread the cover over the dead man's face.

"Yes, sure. Let's move on. Still waiting by the reception area."

"Okay, let's speak to them." Lerato and Johan strolled over to the small group of people waiting inside the reception area.

While Lerato and Johan Phaladi spoke to the

action cricket team, Charlie walked around, listening, looking here and there. Lerato let her be. Charlie had a special gift and looked at things differently. This different way of looking at things that Charlie called intuition was the very reason she wanted to work on murder cases with her.

Charlie perceived their surroundings differently and this often took murder cases in a different direction – and very fast. And they had solved every one of their cases so far.

*

An hour later, they were nearly done with the interviews.

"So, what do you know about John Bhengu's recent activities? Did he have enemies within the company?"

those were the last questions they asked the whole team. It was clear that they wouldn't get much out of these people as time progressed.

They would interview them one by one and the other employees tomorrow morning, then move on to Hannah Bradlow's neighbours.

"Thank you, ladies and gentlemen," Johan Phaladi

released the tired bunch into the night. When the members of the cricket team had left, it was past midnight.

"There goes my early night with a good book," Lerato complained to Charlie as they walked back to the car.

"Yeah well. I also thought I would be spending the rest of the evening chatting to Jono over a cup of tea." Charlie yawned.

"That's not half as much fun as going out on a double date, I suppose. Tell me more about your date earlier. Where did you go?" Lerato pushed the murder case to the side. "I need some distraction from all this."

"We went to that new restaurant on Sandton Square…" Charlie began.

"Piccachu?" Lerato asked.

"Yup." Charlie nodded. "Food was good and we had a great view from the rooftop area, but as I said, I got the impression that Karen – the new inspector, who's by the way, everything but nice didn't like me very much. Always had to get a leg up on me, no matter what I said. She always knew better."

Lerato gave the security guard a sign. He carefully

followed their movements before opening the large gate with his remote control. The gate rolled sluggishly to the side and they were back on the street. A well-lit street this time. The earlier power outage seemed to be over.

"I don't really know her. We spoke on the phone a couple of times," Lerato said. "Sounds bitchy, though."

"Not too bad, but Jono and Karen didn't click right away. Marius and Karen seem to have an easier time chatting with each other. About work, mostly."

"You said. So, you never had that cosy chat with our good inspector…Karen did."

"Well, I still like him and he seemed clueless."

"Like most men." Lerato turned the steering wheel sharply to the left.

"I guess. In any case, he said he might be driving down to the coast with his ex and his daughter meeting family in East London over Christmas. So let's see what happens when he comes back in January. You'll be the first to know."

"At least something…" Lerato said and changed the subject. "Did you pick up on anything around the crime scene? You know…"

Charlie knew what Lerato referred to: anything that her intuition could detect.

"Yeah, not at first. Then while you and Johan were speaking to the action cricket team, I did pick something up. I'll speak to you about it tomorrow morning."

"Why not tell me now?" Lerato asked slightly annoyed.

"I'm tired and it's better to sleep on it or I might forget something important. I'll give you a call." Charlie yawned as if to accentuate the fact that she was tired and closed her eyes.

"Fair enough," Lerato said and drove through the near-empty streets of Johannesburg.

*

Charlie was dreaming she could fly. Like an eagle between hills, carried up by soft, warm air. She was aware of dreaming but felt so free and easy... when her cell phone played the familiar ring tone. She knocked over her bedside lamp as she reached for it.

"Damn!" Charlie muttered. There was something important to her dream, but now she couldn't remember what it was and would probably never know.

"Morning sleepy head!" Lerato crowed cheerfully.

"Hey you eager beaver," Charlie held the phone away from her ear and yawned extensively. "I said I was going to call you."

"Sorry, I couldn't wait any longer," Lerato continued. "So what was it you wanted to tell me about the case yesterday?" Lerato asked. "You know… what you saw."

She had apparently been doing paperwork at the office and was bursting with curiosity. Charlie, on the other hand, had gone to bed late after talking to Jono, who'd waited up for her. Their chat over two cups of rooibos tea had turned from lively to listless when they had gone to sleep.

"So, what did you see at the crime scene? Was it a ghost or vapour or something else, like before? Of course, it was. That's what it usually is, isn't it? Is he going to help us?"

"Lerato, talk slowly… wait I'll phone you back in a minute."

"Wait…" Lerato objected, but Charlie had already hung up and yawned again.

She felt hot, even barefoot and in her oversized t-shirt as she traipsed on the cool tiled floor into the kitchen. She needed to get her bearing before she could face the world. Even Lerato.

Jono had already fed the dogs and was reading the morning paper spread out on the kitchen table. "Finally you're up," he snickered.

"Good morning to you, too." Charlie didn't feel like a hot beverage and poured herself a glass of water and mixed it with orange juice in the jug on the table instead. "What time is it?"

"Almost 10 o'clock," he answered.

"What? Why didn't you wake me up?" She complained.

"You were out, sleepy head… and it's not like you have to go to work or anything. I on the other hand had to test some software…"

The dogs stormed up the three steps into the kitchen, tired of their lively play in the garden to greet Charlie. Their favourite game was a tug of war with a chewed up piece of rope. All other toys were immediately ripped to shreds.

"Okay, okay, you little rascals. Feeling normal after your injections, I see."

Charlie sat down and took a sip of the orange juice.

"If anything, they are even bouncier than usual," Jono answered on their behalf and folded the newspaper with a crackling noise. "Our nasty neighbours were a no-show this morning, so the doggies played outside the whole time."

"Oh… I wonder what's keeping them from tormenting the neighbourhood today. They had to cut their party short, because of the power failure."

Charlie drank up thirstily. "Boy - is it just me or is it damn hot this morning?" She poured herself another glass.

"The forecast is 35°C with scattered thundershowers in the afternoon. That's around 95°F, isn't it? Wonder if I can ever get used to the Celsius system here…"

"Mhm, I felt the same way when we went to America. In the beginning, I couldn't get used to feet and ounces, pounds and yards and stuff like that either. Still doesn't make much sense to me," Charlie yawned.

"Better than British measurements like stone and even their pounds are different to ours," Jono grunted.

He turned the page with a rustling noise and smoothed the newspaper. A habit of his Charlie had gotten used to.

"True. Did you have breakfast?" Charlie asked her brother.

"Emm yeah, it's after 10 o'clock."

"Oops that reminds me, I need to phone Lerato back…" Charlie put her empty glass down.

"Should I make you scrambled eggs so long?" Jono wanted to know.

"Thank you, you're the bestest brother ever."

"Anytime, sis." Jono grinned and walked to the refrigerator to take out the eggs and some milk. His special recipe.

The dogs settled into their baskets and watched the siblings' every move. Billie yawned, which prompted Charlie to yawn again. Lerato answered the phone.

'Hi there, it's me,' she said.

'You sound really awake now,' Lerato chuckled. "Still yawning?"

'Yeah, believe it or not, I am. Sort of.' Charlie poured herself another glass of watered-down juice. 'Maybe coffee wouldn't be such a bad idea this morning.'

Jono tipped his forehead with two fingers and turned on the kettle.

'Do you want to talk over the phone or face to face?" Lerato inquired. "I could meet you somewhere. Already went to the coroner and had another look at our victim. I just hope that our electricity won't go off again. They announced load shedding stage 1 by us in about an hour. Just finishing up the last folder here then we could meet.'

'Hmm, Jono is making me scrambled eggs. Do you want to come over to our place?'

'I can. Alright, give me fifteen minutes. Boy, it's hot. The air-conditioning in our building is off and I'm boiling. God knows how long it will take management to get it fixed. All I have is the desk fan. Florence is lucky, sitting downstairs in the cool lobby.'

'Then load shedding won't make much of a difference anyway.'

'Yeah, just you gloat. Your electricity won't go off until tonight.'

'Really? I haven't checked the app yet, but I'm planning to go to bed early.'

Jono scoffed in the background.

'My dearest brother doesn't seem to believe me.' Charlie glowered at him.

'Don't make any plans for tomorrow. We're going to a Christmas party in the afternoon.'

'A Christmas party?' Charlie was surprised. 'Do we have time for that?'

'Yes, it's at MultoPharm. We finished our interviews yesterday and can go over the notes. The polygraph test is taking place today. If we go to the party, we can suss out the people at the company a bit more. John Bhengu's funeral is next week and we should get moving on the case.'

'Only you and me?'

'Johan will also be there. Pity that the ghosts aren't cooperating this time.'

'Well, they must have their reasons. Might still come through for us. At the Christmas party, maybe.'

'That would be a good thing. I'll see you a bit later.'

'Alright, then see you in a bit.' Charlie rang off.

"Just in time for your breakfast." Jono put a plate with fluffy scrambled eggs in front of his sister and the dogs sniffed the air in greedy delight.

"Thank you so much, bro," Charlie said and made short shrift of the eggs.

"Maybe you guys should go outside and sit under the trees in the back. It's shady and cooler than inside."

"You're right, that'll be cooler there. I wish I could go back to sleep, though."

"It's unusual that you're that tired. Any dream you'd like to discuss?"

"Actually yes. Strange, but I can't remember much of my dream. I was flying and I know it had something to do with this case, but then my cell phone went off and it just flew right out of my head."

"Sounds like a lofty dream. You should tell Lerato about that. I'll make myself scarce now. Getting back to work in the cottage to the drone of my standing fan. Let's see how the test turned out."

There was hooting at the gate and the dogs charged down the driveway to greet Lerato.

They discussed their approach at the crucial Christmas party and the interviews in the shade of the big tree while sipping ice tea and Billie and Popcorn played tug-of-war with their toys.

Chapter FIVE

The Christmas party at the MultoPharm Corporation was held in one of the conference rooms on the ground floor.

The large conference table had been pushed from the middle of the room against the wall and served as a space for paper cups and plates. An area to the left had been cleared of surplus chairs and flip charts to make space for a dance floor and the chairs were lined up around the room.

A group of women were half-sitting on the smooth edge of the heavy conference table, having a lively chat. Most of the men were outside.

The braais on the back lawn were in full swing while the meat was still waiting in its packaging or marinating away in bowls on a separate table under the roof of the broad veranda. Not far from the sliding doors, a table was bending under the weight of bowls with salads, roast potatoes and other side dishes. Men were scurrying between the meat table and the braais that began to sizzle with drumsticks, steaks and boerewors. Barbecuing was a serious job in South Africa. A men's job.

"No, Andy, that goes onto the vegetarian braai over there," Wynand Ryker, the head of the Accounts Department directed one of his minions to a small grill that looked quite empty compared to the grills with the carnivorous fare. "That's for George's wife."

There would be a Father Christmas appearance, while the braaied goods were served later. So far, everything was going fine.

The walls of the conference room were decorated in festive pine branches and baubles – all plastic, of course - and a large artificial Christmas tree dominated the right side by the big sliding doors. The computer department had sourced the decorations on the Internet.

White foamy Christmas trees, unshapely bells and fantasy snowflakes that belied the hot summer weather, were sprayed on the glass.

At previous Christmas events, staff, select clients and suppliers had partied at fancy restaurants in Sandton and Illovo, where they usually enjoyed lavish buffets and set menu luncheons with an open bar - all tax-deductible, of course.

Last year, a belly-dancing competition among female employees had been the highlight of the drunken celebrations at a Greek restaurant.

But this year, the CEO of MultoPharm, Mr. Buitendacht, had put austerity measures in place, in view of the recent murders of two employees and a decline in profits since the pending court case had made the news.

The police were still busy with their investigation. Video recordings of cars that had entered the premises that day didn't show anything unusual, so it was assumed that John Bhengu's killer had climbed over the palisade fence by the highway. Also, the height of the killer was pegged at 1,70 m by the coroner. In other words, it could have been anyone. A chancer, perhaps, they'd said.

At the last staff meeting, a cancellation proposal was met with resistance and in an attempt to prevent widespread mutiny and, when a cacophony of opinions began to take on a threatening tone, Mr. Buitendacht had decided to go ahead with the celebrations. Many were looking forward to the Christmas party all year, so they would rather cut the duration of the party short.

'Sir, we could celebrate their lives rather than not celebrate at all,' one of the saleswomen had argued with guile. She had already bought a sexy outfit especially for this event and she'd be damned if she didn't get to wear it.

'Christmas will happen no matter what,' the chief chemical engineer had said. 'It's the festive season. We can't change that. And it will save us money in entertaining suppliers and clients in the long run. We need their support now more than ever."

It was a convincing argument, everybody could agree to. Celebrating into the wee hours of the morning seemed somehow inappropriate, after all. He was pleased that yet another problem had been resolved to everybody's satisfaction.

As the day of the party, approached, an air of child-like anticipation hung around the otherwise rather business-like offices. The IT team had somehow kept their efforts at decorating the conference room a secret by keeping the doors to the conference room locked. Spray cans and tinsel were stored in one of the empty filing cabinets. Much to the annoyance of the cleaning staff, who were not allowed in for days on end.

When the doors finally opened to let in the first party-goers, the mood had been subdued at first, but when the music started playing and the free booze flowed, people began to relax.

The recent murders did not exactly add to the cheer and as if that wasn't reason enough, the company's action cricket team had lost to their rivals by three runs in the morning. Nevertheless, the turnout was promising and the free-flowing alcohol helped with the overall mood.

Some of the African staff members had opted not to show up at all for fear that spooks could make a nuisance of themselves. What was scary to these staff member, was of course, exactly what Lerato and Charlie were hoping for.

They arrived about an hour into the festivities, when the braais on the lawn were already smoking away merrily, spreading a delicious aroma. People with champagne glasses and beer bottles in their hands were swaying to the tunes of the playlist the legal department had chosen for the event.

"Everybody got a drink?" John Buitendacht asked in a loud voice. "Good, good. A warm welcome to our illustrious guests and members of staff. Good to see you here today. I am glad and at the same time saddened on this day…"

To kick things off, the CEO had given a heartfelt speech, depicting the Christmas party in the correct light to much nodding and clapping.

After a minute of silence for the murder victims, the music started again and the party started in earnest. Fair enough, they would call it a day at 20:00 this evening, but there were still hours of revelling left.

The glass doors at the back were wide open to let in a warm afternoon breeze and everybody was congregating toward the outdoor space.

Light summer wear was the order of the day. The heat didn't quite gel with Charlie's idea of the American Christmas mood she'd become accustomed to.

In New York, she'd be wearing warm winter clothing. A thick jacket, reindeer beanie and gloves and underneath something knitted in green and red colours. Today, however, her light-blue chiffon dress and Lerato's summer suit were just the right attire for an event in the hot South African climate.

During their last video call, her parents had complained about an approaching blizzard that put everybody on edge. Would they still have electricity? Would they be able to go out into the street?

'Mom, we've been having rolling blackouts here for two weeks. You'll survive,' Charlie had said and Jono laughed, although their adoptive parents didn't see things from a cheerful angle.

'You won't be freezing to death when the power goes out, even in winter,' their adopted father, Itumeleng Morake, scolded. 'Here, we're approaching below zero temperatures. That's not a funny prospect.'

'Right, sorry Dad, but it won't be exactly like in the movie 'A Day After Tomorrow'.'

'God I hope not, son,' Mrs. Morake had sighed.

As it turned out, the blizzard was not as bad as expected and nobody froze to death in their houses. The siblings were relieved that their family would be celebrating Christmas safely in their warm apartment. Charlie was still contemplating if she should take a trip to New York to visit her family between Christmas and the New Year. She dearly missed her parents and two other siblings and hadn't been on Times Square for the New Year's countdown in ages.

In the MultoPharm conference room, an intermezzo of Christmas carols had just made way for lively dance music and, fuelled by gin & tonics and an innocent-looking fruit punch that Mathilda Mayer, the big boss' PA had brought, employees were dancing to happy tunes.

When the two sleuths joined the party, Judith Holland was dancing somewhat stiffly with one of the sales guys to a choppy eighties song.

"That's her," Lerato said to Charlie. They had just arrived at MultoPharm and were surveying the room. "Judith Holland. Her polygraph results were inconclusive, even closer to deception."

"The day is still young," Charlie replied while smiling at inquisitive faces. She was aware that they didn't quite fit in with the staff, clients and suppliers, but that couldn't be helped.

She had a feeling that something was about to happen that would help them with their case, although she couldn't say what it would be.

Meanwhile, Judith tried her best to ignore the curious stares from some of her colleagues. These murders had made a deep impact on her. Last but not least, because she had seen Hannah Bradlow's dead body. Her suppressed fears had bubbled up again, when the polygraph expert, who'd been commissioned by Inspector Phaladi, had tested a number of employees yesterday.

Two of them had been found to be deceptive or inconclusive. Things were so not going her way.

Others, who had been tested, turned out to be clearly truthful during the polygraph test.

Now, that could have all sorts of reasons. The trouble was that Judith had been one of the employees with doubtful results, the other one was one of the security guards. That, of course, aroused suspicion.

The test was to be repeated soon, to clear up the situation, but gossip was burning up the grapevine and she got a concentrated dose of it today.

The security guard in question was off duty and not even here, which made things worse. Everybody seemed to be looking at her. Would this whole thing have an impact on her careful career plans at MultoPharm? It wasn't a good thing - that much was abundantly clear. *Fear… fear*, her heart was singing, while she danced.

Although it would have been the easiest way to avoid all this gossip by not coming to the Christmas party, she needed to make an effort or look even more suspicious.

It killed Judith not to know what was being said behind her back. She tried to smile as soon as she felt a stare or sideways look, but when she focused on the person, they didn't look at her at all. It was maddening and Judith felt that it wasn't her fault at all. This could not be turning out like her last company. It just couldn't. As if she didn't have enough problems already.

A fleeting thought of David and what he might be doing now crossed her mind, but she stuck it out like a trooper and kept dancing to a song she had never liked much, pretending to have fun.

Her dance partner was Joe Kepler, one of the sales guys from the second floor. He had been drinking steadily and didn't seem to notice anything amiss with her. In fact, he seemed infatuated to a point, but that could also be the alcohol.

"Perhaps we should go and have something to eat?" Judith suggested as soon as the song ended and Joe moved a little too close for her liking, trying to understand what she was saying over the noise of the new song. "I said maybe we should go outside and have something to eat…" she repeated.

Joe Kepler nodded and guided Judith by the waist to the open sliding doors. She looked pretty in her fitted summer dress and mid-heel sandals that accentuated the good bits of her fuller figure. Judith had decided to go all out with make-up and had even been to the hairdresser this morning.

Her dark locks were immaculately coiffed for the occasion and it was supposed to make her feel more confident. However, the feeling of dread was not so easy to cover up.

"Hi Barbara," she smiled at one of the interns as they walked past a little slip of a woman in a bright yellow outfit.

"Hi." The intern smiled back coolly and turned to face one of the clients. Joe greeted the man amiably.

He was Joe's account and they chatted for a few minutes, while Barbara looked her up and down then found someone else more fascinating.

John Buitendacht excused himself from the client and his wife he had been talking to. With some luck, the large retail chain he represented would order more stock from MultoPharm in the New Year.

He called out to the somewhat sussled salesman. "Joe, why don't you tell Mr. Meyerhoff here about or quantity discounts…"

Judith Holland had been waiting patiently for her lanky dance partner to finish his conversation, now realised that she had to get the food by herself. He didn't even acknowledge her standing there. *Never mind*, she thought and continued to the outdoor area without him.

Mr. Buitendacht was oblivious to her and simply nodded to his salesman and the client he wanted Joe Kepler to enlighten about quantity discounts. Then he noticed Charlie and Lerato and walked over to greet them.

"Good afternoon, ladies. Thank you so much for coming. This is a most unfortunate situation and I wish I could have cancelled the event…"

Oh, you're lying when you move your lips, Charlie thought. "…but that would have spelt disaster for staff morale", he continued. "I cannot believe that our new chartered accountant could have something to do with those murders. Or our security guard. Judith…" He didn't seem sure of the woman's surname.

"…Holland," Lerato said after a moment's hesitation.

"Yes, right… Judith Holland. She is so wholesome and always friendly to everyone. I appreciate it that you agreed to observe my staff. There must be some mistake. The follow-up tests are on Monday and I hope that it all turns out to be an error. No telling, what this could do to the business…"

"It doesn't mean anything," Charlie tried to calm the waves. "I wouldn't jump to conclusions just yet."

"Yes, yes of course." The tall CEO bowed his head a little.

"Excuse us please," Lerato said. "I see Inspector Phaladi over there by the salad buffet. Please don't draw attention to us. We will talk later." She gave the man a winning smile.

"Yes, yes of course," he repeated. "I'll be over here, in case you need anything. I just hope the weather holds."

"Let's hope for the best," Lerato said and observed the sky for a moment as they left the conference room to join the inspector outside.

What she saw didn't look encouraging. Dark clouds were floating in from the eastern sky. The grey cloud blanket flashed every so often with faint lightening. This was nothing unusual at this time of year. Gauteng was a summer rainfall region after all and December was the height of summer. The party guests seemed oblivious to the fact that a rainstorm was brewing overhead.

On the Highveld, rain during a summer braai was a rather common occurrence and many a picnic and barbecue was interrupted by unexpected downpours.

Only the meat on the barbecues had to be rescued as the table with salads and sides was already under the veranda roof. For now, the untroubled afternoon plodded on and everybody seemed to have a good time.

Mr. Buitendacht gave the client he'd left with Joe Kepler a big smile and strode resolutely past Judith

Holland, who was now chatting to two of her female colleagues. She was holding a paper plate with salads and some mielie pap and sous and occasionally nibbled on her food.

The two women had seemingly decided to keep an open mind about the lie detector test. Judith was not the only one with sketchy results after all and obviously, it was not an exact science. One of the security guards was also scheduled for a re-test. All the same, the accountant could feel her colleagues' reservations under the veneer of confidence.

Damn the polygrapher! Judith thought to herself. He could have just said that the test had to be redone, instead of making such a big deal about it. What about privacy? But nothing remained private or personal in any company for long. The grapevine was alight with rumours at the best of times.

It was okay if somebody else was the centre of work gossip, but it embarrassed her deeply that this time it was her. Would her secret be discovered after all? Judith smiled often at her colleagues and tried to change the subject.

"Oh, I'm not sure I could carry off a dress like

that…" she commented on a woman's short hemline and - as expected - the women jumped on the subject.

"Well, why would you want to draw attention to yourself like that?"

Yes, why indeed? It would be good to have these colleagues on her side or she might end up in another situation like the one that had driven her from KYMP, her previous company.

She noticed the two women, who had been with the police on the night the receptionist had been found in the parking lot.

Charlie and Lerato had stopped on their way to greet Johan Phaladi to hang around the women for a while, hoping to catch useful bits of information, but it was just small talk. Judith Holland and everybody else knew, of course, that the two sleuths and Inspector Phaladi were investigating the murder cases.

"Something's not quite right with this lady," Charlie said and Lerato understood.

She knew that Charlie could see something dark around the attractive accountant, who had been working for MultoPharm only a few weeks. Lerato couldn't see a dark cloud, but she could feel that something was off. Perhaps Ms Holland had witnessed something and was too scared to speak about it. She had been quite cagey during the interviews and smiled way too much.

Soon, Lerato nodded for Charlie to follow her and they joined Johan Phaladi, who was laying into the salads and side dishes with gusto under the veranda roof.

Lerato had checked the personnel files of the two employees after the polygraph test went pear-shaped and she knew that Judith Holland had a complicated history with her last employer. The security guard had moved up from The Western Cape and had an impeccable record.

"Hi Johan. You seem awfully hungry," Lerato said as they approached the inspector. "The potato salad any good?"

"Hello ladies," he answered. "Yip, I don't get food like that often. TV dinners from Woolies mostly. All I need is a microwave." He smacked his lips. "I must say, this salad is delicious." He heaped more of the potato salad onto his plate. "And look at that three-bean salad!"

"Has your wife been starving you lately?" Lerato

chuckled.

"She has a full-time job now, so it's heated TV dinners most of the time."

"That explains it. Anything to report here?" Lerato was alluding to the crowd they had come to observe.

"Nothing yet. Some poor souls seem starved for social interaction, but nothing to do with our murders that stands out." He wiped his mouth with a paper serviette.

"Alright, then we'll mingle a bit, while you're having a moment with the delicious side salads. Make the most of it, tomorrow it's back to TV dinners."

"Looks like the meat might still take a while." The inspector gave the braais a longing look.

"You won't starve, Johan," Charlie laughed. "Have some bean salad."

"Nothing for you?" He wanted to know.

"No, not yet anyway." Lerato answered.

"Oh, the mielie pap looks good." He waved with his fork and the two sleuths sauntered back inside the Christmassy conference room.

The music was softer now and slower and a few dancers were strutting their stuff on the improvised dance floor.

Charlie and Lerato stood close to the Christmas tree and tried to observe the party as covertly as possible. Somebody had switched on the flashing mode of the fairy lights and specks of bright colours were dancing on the faces of party-goers nearby.

"I don't think that Wynand Ryker, the Chief Financial Officer, is here yet. I wanted to have a word with him." Lerato scanned the conference room.

"Mhm." Charlie seemed lost in thought.

"Maybe he's still coming…" Lerato probed, but still no reaction.

"Mhm."

"What's going through your mind, Charlie? Should I do a striptease to liven things up a bit?" Lerato was ready to break out laughing, but her friend seemed distracted.

"Sure."

"You don't listen to a word I'm saying," Lerato said a little louder after she'd tried to revive their conversation for the third time.

"What?" Charlie was obviously still deep in thought. "Did you say something?"

"Charlie… what's going on? A ghost flirting with you from across the room or something?" Lerato became annoyed with her friend.

"What are you talking about?" Charlie creased her forehead.

"You're awfully quiet and you're not listening to anything I say. That's what I'm talking about."

"Oh – sorry. I guess I'm just… a little sad," Charlie admitted.

"Sad? Why?" Lerato felt confused. Charlie had no emotional link to either of the victims, whose murders they were investigating. What could be making her so sad that she didn't listen to her?

"Yes… you see… Colin died in the crash almost three years ago and I'm here, at a party. And he's not."

Colin Proudfoot was Charlie's deceased husband. She had lost him and their unborn child in a car crash just before Christmas in New York. Charlie had survived the accident by the skin of her teeth and her grief had lasted for quite some time.

Christmas time must be especially hard for her.

Lerato felt guilty for not remembering this important fact. "I'm so sorry, Charlie," she gave her a light hug. They were at work after all and a more open display of emotion would have surely aroused suspicion. "Do you want to leave? I'm sure I can hold down the fort with Johan's help."

"No, it's okay. I'm just not in a very festive mood, I guess. Haven't celebrated Christmas for a while."

"That's understandable." Lerato gave her an empathic look. "Aren't you going to New York for the holidays to visit your family?"

"Not sure yet, but Jono offered to stay here to look after the house and feed the dogs if I decided to go. We probably should get away from each other for a little while."

"I'm sure you'd miss your brother, but then again, seeing the rest of your family again would be great."

Charlie looked up. They were here at this party for a reason, not to discuss her private feelings. There was no change in the room. The dark vapour still hung around Judith Holland's head, but other than that, she had not seen anything unusual. "I'm just not sure yet about other things," she said.

"Oh? Is it the cold weather in New York?" Lerato shuddered just thinking of snow. She very much preferred the South African climate.

"It would actually be nice for a change, but … I mean I went on a date with Marius. What was I thinking? "

"Oh, I see. You feel guilty about being interested in other men."

"Yes, exactly. I'm feeling a little confused."

"Charlie, it's been three years. Don't you think it's time that you let go a little bit? I'm sure Colin - whom I've never met - doesn't mind if you try to find love again."

"It was just dinner. Not a marriage proposal."

"Just friendship with a man. You should like people you are friends with. But if you married Colin, he must have been an awesome guy and he would want you to live your best life." Lerato's argument made sense to her. Charlie thought for a moment while the music thumped rhythmically and the lights on the Christmas tree flickered.

"Yes, you're right. I think it's just that time of year again. And Marius' colleague, Karen… I mean she turned the whole thing into some kind of competition. That's not what I want. With Colin things were easy.

He courted me. No jumping through hoops. I wish I could celebrate Christmas with him one last time." Charlie sighed.

A group of people broke out into uproarious laughter. The moment was jarring. The two friends looked in the direction of the sudden noise. The laughter died down quickly, making way for the murmur and music as before.

"In any case, you're not exactly celebrating Christmas here. We are hard at work and you better pay attention to what's going on around you. I rely on your… intuition, and we might not get another chance to observe everybody together."

Lerato didn't mean to sound harsh, but she had to try and snap Charlie out of her dark mood. She watched a man doing awkward dance moves. He made her smile.

"You're right. I shouldn't let this mood take over. Not anymore." Charlie sighed.

"What do you think of that guy over there?" Lerato sniggered.

"What guy?"

Before Lerato could tell her friend, a loud

thunderclap rang out overhead, right above them. It made the two PIs and the other party guests flinch. Then a rumbling noise rolled across the sky and shook the walls of the building. Women shrieked and the conversations died down, but the party guests were only briefly preoccupied with the noise of an approaching thunderstorm.

A few men went outside to investigate, as if they could do anything about stopping the storm. They returned shaking their heads. Apparently, it didn't look like rain just yet.

"The sky's grey and it's raining over there," a man in a green and yellow sports shirt stated expertly. It just smells like rain." He pointed in the direction of downtown Johannesburg.

"You smell the rain, Harold? A rain sniffer dog, we have here," a woman with too much makeup shrieked. Some people laughed at the mocking remark.

"Maybe we'll get a monkey's wedding," another man said. "Sunshine and rain at the same time. Haven't seen that for a while."

"It won't take long before it rains," Charlie said to

Lerato. "I hope that Jono remembers to switch off the main fuse at home."

"You could give him a call."

"Nah, he's quite good with stuff like that. He'll also put the dogs into the kitchen. Popcorn gets nervous during thunderstorms."

A wild dance song came on and the guests were singing along. Some of them were more in tune than the others. A number of people hit the dance floor and gyrated to the music.

Another group of women close by chatted in cautious tones. Lerato was facing them but didn't let on that she was eavesdropping. She started moving to the music as if she couldn't care less about their gossip.

"Yes, and her boyfriend apparently left her. His name is David. He's emigrating to Australia, I think," Mr. Buitendacht's secretary said. She seemed proud of sharing information the others didn't have.

"Really, did she tell you about it?" A woman with buckteeth asked.

"No, one of the holiday temps did. Dani. She is David's sister and Judith Holland got her the job," Mathilda Mayer explained.

"You think, she cracked? I was in a bad way when my boyfriend broke up with me last year."

"I wouldn't be surprised, but she doesn't seem the type to commit murder. Not just one, but two…" another woman in bright pink top said. " That's a bit far-fetched."

"You can't tell from just looking at someone." Mathilda Mayer cautioned. "Let's not spread rumours."

"Of course not," the woman in the pink top said quickly.

Lerato tried to pick up more of the conversation, but the women carried on chatting about other things while sipping on a new round of drinks, one of the men was handing out.

"I think the drinking loosens their tongues," she whispered in Charlie's ear. Surprisingly, her friend had been paying attention.

"In vino veritas," Charlie nodded. "There is truth in wine. I think we need to have a chat with this Dani person."

"I'll say. She's a holiday temp, so she's probably not here." Lerato scanned the room. "We should strike up a conversation with some of the women. They seem happy to gossip given a chance."

"I wouldn't bet on it, but it's worth a try."

Lerato joined another small group of women, who were watching the dancers, while Charlie tried to observe what was going on behind the scenes. Something still wasn't right, but what?

The women didn't give out much information about the holiday temp called Dani. Only that she came from Pretoria and studied in Johannesburg.

Lerato laughed at a joke she didn't understand and Charlie chuckled half-heartedly. She ached to get away from all this gossip.

Chapter SIX

It grew darker outside. Clouds blocked out the sun and long shadows in the company gardens jabbed at the lawns. Charlie's attention was drawn to a short, blonde woman, who watched the party from a bench under one of the tall willow trees. She was pale and didn't seem to enjoy the party mood.

"Let me go over there and speak to that woman on the bench," she said to Lerato.

"What woman?" Lerato asked. "Judith Holland?"

Where was Judith Holland? Lerato was unable to spot the accountant in the conference room or outside. Charlie was already on her way past the sliding doors when another thunderclap reverberated around the company building.

She stopped in her tracks. It wasn't a good idea to run across the lawn when the heavens were about to open any minute. But when Charlie looked again, the blonde woman was gone.

"Hey baby, wanna dance?" A balding middle-aged

man tried to pull Charlie onto the dance floor. Judging by his alcoholic breath, he should be barely conscious.

"No thank you," Charlie bellowed and only realised at that moment that the music had suddenly stopped.

The other party guests were eyeballing her. Who was that noisy woman? They got quickly distracted. The lights on the Christmas tree flickered a few times then the room went dark. So did lamps all over the building, but they came back on a minute later.

"Damn. You don't know these days if it's load shedding or the fuses," somebody said and the others murmured approval.

"Or a substation blowing up again," a woman piped up. "Or cable thieves at work."

"Or that. But we're back on now," the CEO said in a calming tone and everybody relaxed. "So keep enjoying yourself." The music started again and the party guests carried on as before.

The sun was now hiding behind a wall of grey clouds. Before they knew it, a strong wind picked up and the dark billowing clouds released a torrent of water. There was more shrieking - less terrified now, but surprised. Rain started pounding the lawn and the veranda roof. Those, who were outside started running for cover.

"Where's our sniffer dog? Harold, can you smell the rain now?" One of the men yelled and laughed raucously. Everyone found that terribly amusing and Harold, who was on the dance floor with his girlfriend started laughing as well.

Plan B kicked in without delay. Busy hands started moving bowls with grilled goods onto a table on the broad veranda. The aroma of the barbecued meats wafted into the conference room and even Lerato felt hungry.

"The meat's done," somebody shouted quite unnecessarily over the noise of the gushing rain. "Come on folks, gather 'round. Grab a plate and line up. Steaks and chops are ready - and our award-winning boerewors, of course. Chicken should be alright, too."

"Hey, who made you the braai master, Gerald?" One of the salesmen quipped.

"Do you want to eat or not?" Gerald retorted and

picked up a piece of meat with metal tongs.

"Alright, alright…"

"Then let's go." Gerald didn't have to say it twice. Party guests were lining up in front of the tables on the veranda while trying to avoid the rain that ran noisily off the roof in broad see-through sheets onto the lawn. The rain had cooled down the summer heat considerably. Excited chatter accompanied the feeding of the carnivores.

"Who put the mielies on the braai?" Gerald shouted.

"They're mine," Elizabeth yelled. "And one of those seitan steaklets is also mine. Am I the only vegetarian here?"

"Looks like it."

"No wait, I'm also vegetarian," George's wife piped up. "Two of them are mine."

"Here you go."

"Okay, slap them on my plate." Elizabeth held her plate out and Gerald let one seitan steak slide onto the smooth cardboard, followed by the grilled corn. Then it was the other vegetarian's turn.

"Next… boerewors or steak?" Gerald began to dish out the barbecued meat.

There were only three people left on the dancefloor. They swung their arms drunkenly back and forth and seemed oblivious to the commotion around them. Their thin bubble burst when the strident sound of hammering rain replaced the music. It was a cold, wet substitute for the pleasant tunes. At the same time, all the lights in the building went out again. This time for good.

The dancers stopped moving and looked around with confused expressions. The flickering fairy lights on the Christmas tree ceased and the room grew still.

Everybody was convinced that the sudden blackout most likely meant yet another unscheduled load shedding event. Residents had become accustomed to the unforeseen electrical blackouts – as frustrating as they were. Luckily, the company had a backup generator that allowed them to run the business off-grid if needed.

The generator would jump into action any moment now. They waited in expectation, but nothing happened. Unbeknownst to them, the cause for the blackout was an entirely different one this time.

After ten minutes, John Buitendacht called his top

salesman Joe Kepler over.

"Joe, go and check what's going on with the generator. It's not kicking in and we need to keep the show going." He snipped his fingers imperiously.

The salesman was eager to please. "Certainly, sir," he said and put his plate with grilled meats at once down on the corner of the conference table. "You stay away from my food," he warned his colleagues, who made snapping gestures at his plate.

"I mean it," he said and they laughed.

Joe Kepler was the CEO's right-hand man in all manner of difficult circumstances. He sprinted off into the long, dark passage to inspect what could possibly keep the generator from doing its job. There were no windows in the passage and the wire-grid glass window in the security door at the end of the passage was literally the light at the end of the tunnel.

The CEO grunted contentedly and greeted another one of his important clients with an amiable pat on the shoulder.

"Enjoying yourself, Dean?"

The man nodded and lifted his glass. "Apart from the load-shedding… I heard that Father Christmas and some elves will be making an appearance."

"Now where would you hear something like that? Although a real Christmas party without Father Christmas wouldn't be worth its salt," John Buitendacht said.

The man chuckled. "Indeed, indeed." He was hoping for sparsely clad female elves and smacked his lips. Curious eyes were staring at them and John Buitendacht could feel the party mood drop like a rock.

"Come on, people – nobody with a downloaded playlist on their phone? Light some candles. And the drinks are only getting cold over there at the bar."

The CEO knew how to take charge in a difficult situation. He wasn't CEO of MultoPharm for nothing. The party guests laughed and moved over to the bar. Somebody held up his cell phone that emitted faint music. 'Happy, shiny people holding hands…'

The song echoed in the passage when Joe Kepler reached the security door. He could hear that the rain was letting up somewhat. Good, that would make his job easier. He unlocked the door with his access card, still humming the catchy tune of the last song before the power went off, and saw the top of the rather hefty machine that was located under a roof just outside the building.

He opened the security door and froze in his tracks.

Joe Kepler couldn't believe his eyes.

At the bottom of the generator, Julius Mandel the company lawyer lay across the thick sturdy pipe with cables that ran underground into the company building.

It was obvious that the middle-aged man with the receding hairline had somehow been electrocuted. Possibly a crack in the plastic pipe that exposed the cables inside.

His golf shirt had burn marks on them and so did his hand that was hanging down by his side. A soggy pink notepaper and a pen were submerged in the puddle underneath.

The lawyer's feet were still planted at an angle on the concrete slab that stuck out from the dripping wet grass. The dead man stood in a shallow puddle that had formed on the slab during the downpour.

Through the pouring rain, Joe Kepler could hear a soft sizzling noise.

The shocked salesman was struggling to understand what he was looking at. He pushed down the door stop and looked again.

The head of the legal department had been happily eating lamb chops only a few minutes ago, hadn't he? And now, he was obviously dead. Electrocuted.

The realisation hit the salesman like a sucker punch. Just what's Julius doing out here? It was the last thought going through Joe Kepler's mind before he lost consciousness, sliding down the passage wall with one foot still outside the door.

*

When he came to, his colleagues were leaning over him. "Joe… Joe…" Gerald slapped him again across the face and stared into his eyes.

"Hey, what are you doing that for?" Joe Kepler murmured in an annoyed tone and grunted.

"Oh good, he's alright," Gerald told the rest of the party crowd, who were piling into the passage behind him, rubbernecking. He was the designated First Aid person at the company and had taken charge of the situation, the minute they had found Joe Kepler sitting against the wall.

The salesman hadn't returned from his errand that's why John Buitendacht had sent three other men to investigate. Joe Kepler pointed outside and they'd discovered the body draped over the generator. The party guests had the good sense not to go near the puddle or the dead man, which was astounding, considering their varying stages of drunkenness.

Not much later, Inspector Johan Phaladi was already scrutinising the murder scene from the safety of the much smaller concrete slab in front of the security door.

He had borrowed a wooden broom from a cupboard in the hall and retrieved the wet pink paper slip and the pen from the puddle.

A couple of people pushed up against him to catch a glimpse and he stepped onto the grass after deciding that it would be safe to do so.

"Nobody else goes outside. This thing is dangerous," John Buitendacht shouted at them and they moved back. "Did somebody call the electrician?"

"Your damn luck you didn't go outside, Joe, or you'd be in the same way as poor old Julius." Somebody in a Father Christmas costume said.

Two shivering girls in elf-costumes tried to catch a look while hiding behind his back. They had been handing out little bags with biscuits earlier in the conference room, just before Joe Kepler and Julius Mandel were discovered.

"What?" Joe Kepler asked groggily.

"Don't you remember? Julius is out there by the generator," Gerald said.

"Julius? Oh yes." Joe held his hand in front of his eyes.

"Maybe he hit his head," a woman suggested and gave him a curious look.

"Yeah, that's possible. Check the back of his head."

"Where's the ambulance? And the security company?" John Buitendacht asked. "You should stay here with Joe, Gerald… and why don't the rest of us go back to the party room? There's nothing we can do here. If the police show up, send them over to me."

Reluctantly, the crowd began to move backwards then returned slowly to the conference room, some of them sobering up, some laying into the remaining alcohol reserves at the bar.

"Gee John, is this becoming a pattern here? What's

going on at MultoPharm?" One of the suppliers asked the company's CEO, while he walked alongside him.

The dark passage was illuminated only by cell phone screens. Nobody had been allowed to take pictures of the scene, but everybody had brought their phones along.

The supplier was, of course, referring to the killings of two staff members with the third murder victim obviously now lying dead outside on a generator.

"Morné, what can I tell you. We are all in shock here. Somebody obviously means harm to my people…"

"If I was you, I wouldn't rely on the police, John. Why don't you get private detectives involved? I'm sure they'll get you results much faster. Honestly, if it was my company, I would hire a private investigator."

"Already done, Morné." John Buitendacht looked around and saw Lerato and Charlie. The crowd was pushing past them in the opposite direction as they tried to reach the security door.

"Ms Gwala, could you come here for a moment?" He called out to the PI.

"Mr. Buitendacht…" Lerato picked her way around departing party guests.

"This is Morné Kriel, one of our esteemed suppliers. Would you please tell him, what you are doing here?"

The ambulance had arrived and paramedics made their way past them to reach Joe Kepler, who was still sitting on the floor. They stepped aside and the CEO of MultoPharm planted himself in front of the two private detectives.

"Mr. Buitendacht, do you think it's wise…" Lerato began, but the CEO interrupted her, eager to appease his supplier.

"No, no it's fine, Ms Gwala. Mr. Kriel here is worried about the state of affairs at MultoPharm and needs to know that we are making every effort to solve the murders."

"Well, in that case, sir. I'm Lerato Gwala of the Maitirelo Private Investigation Agency and this is my associate, Charlotte Proudfoot. We are here to investigate the murders at MultoPharm, in collaboration with the police so to speak. And we must now assess the situation outside, if you don't mind. Please excuse us, we would like to lend Inspector Phaladi outside a hand."

She turned around and the two women headed for the security door, where the paramedics checked on Joe Kepler's blood pressure before placing him on a stretcher and taking him away to the waiting ambulance.

"Hi, Johan…" Lerato said quietly. "What's going on?"

The rain had stopped for the moment.

"Don't touch the concrete slab," the inspector said in a warning tone and walked toward them across the lawn. The rain had stopped and the sun peeked out from behind the fading clouds. "Poor guy, the chief company lawyer, must have touched a live wire. Must have died of a strong electric shock. The electricians should be here any moment."

"Any idea, what the victim was doing by the generator and what happened?"

"Victim's name's Julius Mandel, head of the legal department. Possibly had a rendezvous out here. Found a blank note in a puddle. He's holding on to another pink notepaper in his fist. Possibly touched the note stuck next to the live wire. We'll have to wait for the electrician to shut everything off. Apparently, nobody at the company seems to know how to do that."

"So you think that the note was placed for him to find?"

"Too soon to call. I can't make out what's written on the note in his hand." The inspector shrugged his shoulders. "But the paper's still intact."

"A tryst, maybe. It's not unheard of that people hook up at parties," Charlie suggested. She felt chilly in her light summer dress.

"You mean a woman?" Johan Phaladi looked up.

"Believe it or not, but it could also be a man. Who knows which way he was swinging," Lerato said.

"Yes, of course, but as I said, it's too soon to call." The inspector joined them on the concrete landing just outside the security door. "We need to read the note in his hand first.

"How come you didn't' get shocked?" Charlie asked him.

"Insulation. There's no direct connection between the concrete and the grass. The slab is supposed to isolate the generator from the surroundings and the roof protects it from the elements. The wind must have driven the rain on top of the slab, that's why there are puddles."

"Why would he step onto the platform and touch the generator?" Lerato mused. "If this was a murder, it's quite an elaborate plan."

"Who knows, could have been an accident. Maybe he was just keen to find out what was written on that note and it wasn't a planned murder at all."

"I'm surprised that the paper didn't burn," Charlie said.

"Probably too moist for that. Nothing's written on the note in the puddle. Must have fallen down by accident."

"And how did the person, who placed the note he's holding not get electrocuted?"

"Sheer luck I guess, especially if he or she stuck it there before the storm broke," Lerato said.

"I just don't understand how the perp could have known that it would start raining at the time Mr. Mandel reached the generator." Charlie looked around but saw nothing out of the ordinary. Lerato picked up on her gaze.

"I'm sure we'll figure it out. Where's the damn

electrician?" The inspector checked the passage, but no sign of the man of the hour.

"He'll be here soon, I'm sure," Lerato said and followed Charlie inside when it started to drizzle. Ten minutes later, the electrician arrived with an assistant and had the situation under control in no time.

The initial inspection proved the theory that Mr. Mandel's death was not accidental. The crumpled note they retrieved from his deeply burned hand, had been folded over after the words 'I'm behind the'…

"I need to bag this," the inspector said and found a sandwich bag in the inner pocket of his jacket, where the silicon gloves had come from. "Now, we're waiting for CSI. Great, that's not how I'd imagined a Christmas party with good food to pan out."

"Are you seriously complaining about that? You're at work after all," Lerato scolded him.

"I know. Sorry, but I really would have enjoyed the braai."

Lerato gave him a wilting look then she chuckled. "It's alright, Johan, I was just teasing. I mean, who could have known that there'd be another murder victim today."

"It must be quite risky to plan a murder with all those party guests hanging around. Even with the music and all," the inspector mused.

"Maybe the murder wasn't planned," Charlie said. "Or not planned like that."

"What do you mean?" Lerato asked.

"Well, the other victims were stabbed and pushed off a height. Our man here was electrocuted. So either it was a different killer or it wasn't how things were supposed to go down. Just a thought." Charlie shrugged her shoulders.

"You mean the cracked pipe and the live wire were just a fluke? But what's the point of luring Julius Mandel out to the generator in the first place?"

"Maybe that's where they usually meet?" Charlie wasn't sure how to back up her theory. She just had a feeling and that wasn't easy to explain.

"Right, why not. That's not the worst scenario." Lerato was puzzled by this new angle to the story.

"The cable was frayed and too close to the crack in the plastic casing. The note was left before the rain started. That much seems clear," Inspector Phaladi summarised. "How can we establish the facts, unless there was a witness?"

"The person, who left the note? Or HE was the one, leaving the note," Lerato suggested. "And got electrocuted in the process of leaving it."

"That would make less sense, but everything is possible at this stage," the inspector said.

"Did you check his pockets?" Charlie asked on a hunch.

"No, I wanted to let CSI do that," the inspector answered. "Oh, what the heck."

He walked over to the generator. The drizzle had died down.

Julius Mandel was still in the same position as before. Just that the odd sizzling sound had stopped.

Since it was now safe to approach the body, Johan Phaladi rifled through the dead man's jacket pockets and pulled out a pink note with the scribbled words 'meet me by the generater'. The word generator was misspelt and trailed off to the right. Maybe it had been written in a hurry.

He showed his find to Charlie and Lerato then put it in the sandwich bag with the other note.

"I'll wait for the CSI team, but you could start asking

questions in there. The party is over in any case."

"If we get lucky, we might even find a pink notepad," Lerato said.

*

They didn't find the notepad, which was of a sort that was widely used all over the office building, but there were some interesting clues in the recordings. They played them back at the Maitirelo offices in Parktown North.

'… yes I did see it with my own eyes. She whispered something to Julius Mandel and then gave him something.'

'Did you see either of them walk out of the conference room?' Lerato asked in the recording of the interview with Mathilda Mayer, the CEO's secretary.

'I wouldn't know,' she answered in a pesky tone. 'I mean, I didn't watch them intentionally, of course.'

'Of course not, Ms Mayer,' Lerato could be heard saying. 'I'm not trying to imply that you did, but any little detail might help.'

'Well, I remember that Judith Holland walked out briefly. I assumed that she had to go to the loo, but I can't say for sure. And Julius, I was busy chatting to some colleagues, so I didn't see him leave the room at all.'

"Could you say at more or less what time Ms Holland went to the… loo? I mean was it before or after the lights went off?' Lerato asked.

The secretary thought for a moment. 'I think it was before the lights went off, but again, I can't be sure.'

'Would you be able to say if it was a long time before the lights went off?' Lerato dug deeper.

'Hmm, I'd say yes, but as I said, I didn't watch her…'

'Of course, you didn't. Thank you very much, Ms Mayer. You've been a great help.'

Lerato stopped the recording.

"What would we do without nosy gossip-mongers like her?" The inspector said and took a sip from the water bottle in his hand. The air-conditioning in the building was still off and the temperature in the office was uncomfortably hot. He'd opened the top buttons of his shirt and loosened his tie. His jacket was hanging neatly over the back of the chair he was sitting on.

"Indeed," Lerato agreed.

They had listened to all the interviews, but this one was the most interesting piece of the puzzle.

"What do you think of Judith Holland's interview?"

"She seems to have something to hide, but what and why? It's not unusual to go to the loo or even to pass a note to a colleague, but under the circumstances, we should definitely have another word with her."

"Why on earth did we waste time with all the other witnesses? This secretary seems to know what's going on at all times," Johan Phaladi took another sip of water.

"Do you think that the live wire caused the blackout?" Charlie wanted to know.

"I asked the electrician the same question and he said that it's more likely that the generator tripped again after the first blackout because the transfer switch automatically starts the generator and the interlock shuts off the mains."

"What does that mean?" Charlie asked.

"I can't explain it any better." Johan Phaladi scratched his ear.

"Hmm, I have no idea what it means." Lerato

rolled her eyes. "And I know zilch about electrical appliances and stuff like that, but the electricity came back on the first time around. Either somebody switched it back on or it came on by itself."

"Hmm. Hard to say," Johan Phaladi said. "That type of standby generator only comes on when there's already a loss of electricity from the grid. I'm also no expert, but the electrician pointed out that the trees hadn't been trimmed around the power lines and might have caused the first blackout when the wind picked up."

"Is that possible?" Lerato wondered.

"Apparently, under certain circumstances."

"It kind of makes sense, though," Charlie said. "That could have caused the generator to kick in. Normally, the cracked pipe wouldn't have caused a problem, but with the puddle and Mr. Mandel touching the spot… the short in the generator might have caused only the secondary blackout, then."

"Great, then we're on square one… our perpetrator couldn't possibly have known all of this. So it was unlikely a planned murder." Lerato shrugged.

"That would support the theory that the

electrocution wasn't planned as such. Perhaps it was just a matter of being in the wrong place at the wrong time."

"Okay, where does that leave us?" Charlie asked.

"We'll find out. We'll ask more questions and you'll work your magic," Lerato winked at her friend.

Charlie was a little concerned about the fact that neither of the murder victims had introduced themselves in spirit form yet. This was unusual, compared to the other cases they had worked. She couldn't imagine the reason for it, except that her 'magic' wasn't working this time.

They had questioned the families of the murdered MultoPharm employees before this last incident. If they could be believed, the victims had no obvious enemies nor were they involved in any extraordinary activities. Nobody could offer an explanation why they had been targeted, except that Johannesburg, in general, was a paradise for criminals and it had to hit closer to home at some stage.

It wasn't unusual that family members would keep information from the police to protect a murder victim's reputation, but where did it leave their investigation?

Lerato roused herself.

"Okay, so we still have two candidates for follow-up interviews. This holiday temp called Dani Coetzee, the sister of Judith Holland's ex-boyfriend and the lady herself."

"Don't forget the other staff member, who failed the lie detector test. Herbert Tuins. We should also question him again."

"Yes, of course, three then."

Lerato stood up and got herself a glass of water at the sink. "Too bad I haven't got any water bottles left in the fridge. Anyone else?"

"I'll have some water, thanks," Charlie said and Lerato poured another glass.

"But he wasn't at the party," Johan Phaladi continued. "Either this company is extremely unlucky or we have a serial killer on our hands. Do you ladies want to take the women and I'll speak to Mr. Tuins? It's the weekend, so I assume that none of them will come to work today."

"Deal. I have their contact details. Here is Mr. Tuins' phone number and address."

He took the note from Lerato and studied it. "He lives in Eldorado Park. Maybe I should rather go with one of my sergeants."

"Judith Holland has an apartment in Killarney and Dani Coetzee stays in res at the university. I think we should try her first. Her parents live in Pretoria and with the holidays coming up, she might move back home soon."

"I think the schools are breaking up on Tuesday," Charlie said.

"How do you even know these things?" Lerato laughed.

"I read the news." Charlie grinned. Her brother Jono strangely preferred the newspaper to online news and they sometimes discussed current affairs.

"I probably should, too, but with all that work on my desk, I have little time for that," Lerato said.

"Well, you should tell Andy off. You're working way too hard. It's his company as well," Charlie complained.

"You know what it's like. His new family is keeping him on his toes."

"How long is that excuse gonna stick?" Charlie murmured. "But it's your call. If you think you can handle it all, then you won't have time to read the news."

"Yeah, I know… " Lerato sighed.

The inspector stood up and peeled his jacket off the chair. "Okay ladies, I'll be on my way. Thanks for the water. I thought the rain would cool temperatures down today, but we're in for more heat, it seems."

"Alright, let's touch sides tomorrow then, after the interviews."

"With some luck, I'll be able to watch the cricket match against Australia tomorrow," the inspector said. "Bummer, I'll miss the first day."

"Well, not that I remember much about cricket," Charlie replied. "But I hope South Africa wins."

"Yeah, so do I. The chances of that are good. Read it in the news." He winked at them and picked up his car keys.

Chapter SEVEN

Judith Holland's apartment was situated in the suburb of Linden, on the second floor of a four-storey building, surrounded by lush green gardens.

It was one of the cheaper apartment buildings in the area. They could hear the TV, while they were waiting for Ms Holland to ask them in. The first day of the cricket match was on and one of the teams must have scored massively.

"Do you mind if we ask you a few questions?" Lerato asked the barefoot brunette, who opened the door for them. She was dressed in a casual pair of shorts and a black camisole top.

"Ms Gwala, isn't it?" Judith Holland asked. "You work with the police."

"Yes, may we come inside? You'll remember my associate, Ms Proudfoot."

Judith Holland's eyes darted over to Charlie, who nodded a friendly greeting before she opened the door with an inviting gesture. "Please come in," she said politely and stepped aside. She knew, of course, why the two women were calling on her and it made her nervous.

"Thank you."

Lerato and Charlie entered the apartment and stared at themselves in the passage mirror opposite the entrance. The effect resulted in a short awkward silence. The accountant led the way into the small lounge.

"I hope you don't mind that I have the TV on. It's the cricket match against Australia. Everybody at the office is watching it and I need to be able to talk about it on Monday morning. Wait, I'll turn the volume down."

She walked over to the flat-screen TV and pressed the volume button a few times. The announcer was now a soft whisper in the background.

"Please have a seat."

The women sat down on the two-seater couch, while their hostess took the easy chair.

"Where are my manners," she said with her eyes on the TV screen. "Can I offer you something to drink?"

"No thank you, Ms Holland. We just have a few questions," Lerato said as she had so many times before.

"Yes of course. I assume it is about the death of our manager."

"Well, yes mainly. But perhaps you could also enlighten us about the other two murders that happened before Saturday."

"Me? What more can I tell you about that? I've already answered questions by the police – and by you."

"It's just that… there are a few discrepancies we would like to clear up." As so often, Lerato did most of the talking, while Charlie studied the room and Judith Holland in particular.

The lounge was simply furnished with an outdated couch and curtains that had possibly belonged to her parents. Not unusual for a start-up place.

A few plants languished in flowerpots on the window sill. The garden behind the building, however, was in full bloom.

As so often, it was shared by all the tenants. She could see a young woman push a pram toward one of the benches, sit down and tend to her baby.

On the cabinet, next to the TV screen were a few photographs of elderly people and a young man with a short beard. He was stocky and quite ordinary looking.

One of the pictures showed Judith Holland and the young man laughing directly at the camera. In another photo, they sat around a smoking braai in front of a hut somewhere in the bushveld with a group of young people.

A holiday with friends, no doubt.

This must be the ex-boyfriend, Charlie thought. *Odd that she hasn't taken his photos down.*

According to his sister, Dani, David Coetzee was preparing to travel to New Zealand after Christmas. Another woman, a family friend, he was planning to marry on the spur of the moment, would follow him to Wellington in March.

Dani Coetzee had revealed that Judith Holland was heartbroken when she'd been given the news of the impending marriage. Who wouldn't be? But Judith Holland was a good sport and had still organised Dani's holiday job at MultoPharm. That was big of her.

Charlie was sure that everybody at the company

knew Judith's business, but none of her colleagues had mentioned her precarious personal situation during the interviews. Neither had she. This put things somewhat in perspective.

At work, the diligent accountant had seemed unaffected by the breakup. Dani had worried that David's plans could have a negative influence on their relationship at the company, but Judith just smiled when their paths crossed and behaved in a pleasant enough manner.

It seemed a little creepy, though, that Judith took it so well after the initial melt-down. She saw her quite often because Dani had to drop off mail at the different offices, including the Finance Department, where Judith worked.

According to Dani Coetzee, things were fine.

Her brother's ex-girlfriend even got her a Christmas party invitation, but Dani had something else on that day and couldn't make it. Now she was glad that she hadn't come.

Just imagine… another murder. Lucky that she only had a few days of work left, the young woman had said and shook herself. Poor Judith had to work there and who knew… she might be next on the killer's list.

Yet, Charlie still saw a dark cloud around Judith Holland and had no explanation for it - at least not yet. Meanwhile, Lerato conducted the interview in her usual, professional manner.

"Yes, as I said before," the woman answered her question. "Hannah Bradlow wasn't at home when I tried to drop off some documents she had requested that day. So I left. That's all I can tell you."

"Did you notice anything unusual? Was the door to her apartment open? Did you see someone around or did you hear unusual noises?"

"No, not when I left. It was strange that she didn't open the door. We had an appointment, but she was clearly not in the apartment." Should she tell them about the man? The neighbour she had seen disappear through a door on the same floor where Hannah had lived? She decided against it.

Charlie saw how thin vapour swirled around behind the accountant and she gave Lerato a quizzical look. Even without a polygraph test, she could tell that there was something the woman was hiding from them.

"Yes, that's what you said before, but during the polygraph test, you were asked if you knew anything about the killing and your answer was found to be… deceptive. Perhaps you should tell us the truth?" Lerato came to the point.

"I can't really explain it," Judith sighed. "First I thought there must be something wrong with the machine, but I guess it has to do with the dream I had."

"What dream?" Lerato asked and Charlie pricked her ears.

"Well you see, I had this nightmare a couple of nights after Hannah was found and I saw her falling from a window and landing on a lawn. She sat huddled on the lawn with a knife sticking out of her back. I was terribly frightened and woke up."

"A nightmare?" Lerato looked at Charlie.

Judith shrugged her shoulders. "Yes, a nightmare where I could see Hannah on a piece of lawn with a knife in her back. A scary dream and it kept coming back."

"Why do you think you would dream about something like that? Lerato asked.

"I don't know why. I didn't tell anybody, of course. I mean that's not something you can share with people. I can't really explain it. Maybe I'm psychic."

"So you think you are psychic and that fact that you dreamed about the murder victim could have been picked up by the polygraph as an actual incident?"

Judith Holland shrugged her shoulders. "What else could it be?"

Lerato creased her forehead and glanced at her friend. Was this for real?

"Has this sort of thing happened to you before with other events? That you dreamed about them, I mean?" Charlie asked her.

"Hmm, come to think of it, yes it has. Like when our puppy fell into the pool and drowned. Everybody thought it was me, but I wasn't even near the pool when it happened. I was reading a book and I dreamed about the poor little sod going under over and over again later. His name was Wiggle."

"I see. And what about the other murder victims?"

Judith looked almost scared now. "Anybody would

have nightmares after seeing that. My GP already put me on Lexamil, because of what happened at my old company. So it's easier to deal with this stress, but I still get the occasional nightmares. Hannah is giving me the worst nightmares, though."

She looked up to her left as if she was seeing what happened right in front of her eyes. Was Judith lying?

"I'm sure that some of your colleagues also suffered from nightmares after the murders, yet during the lie detector test, only two were found to be deceptive. And you are one of them."

"I told you - that's the only reason I can think of why it happened. My dreams are probably just so real that the machine picked it up. That's not my fault."

"So you think you might be psychic?" Charlie probed again.

"Well, how else would you explain that I dream of these murders and then it shows up on the test?" The white of her eyes was showing and she played with the tassels on the couch cover.

"You tell me," Charlie said.

"You don't believe me?" Judith knitted her eyebrows.

"Should I?" Charlie answered evasively.

She saw a faint vapour rising up behind the woman again that stood in stark contrast to the dark halo around her. That's what she'd been waiting for. *Give me more*, she thought intensely, *give me more*.

"Should you believe me? Of course, you should, because I'm telling the truth." Judith seemed upset now. She locked eyes with the American woman. How dare she?! Judith thought violently.

"Alright," Lerato said. "Let's assume that you are psychic. Then tell us, who you think might be behind those murders."

Judith Holland broke out in a sweat. On the outside, however, she tried to appear as cool as a cucumber. "I'm not THAT psychic. I just tried to explain that I might have failed the lie detector test because of my nightmare."

"Could you explain then, what the note you gave to Julius Mandel at the party was all about? The pink note. We have witnesses."

"I see. He couldn't understand what I was saying to him, because the music was too loud. He needed some figures, so I wrote them down for him. That's all."

This woman seemed to have an answer for everything.

"But we didn't find another note."

"Oh, I don't know… he must have thrown it away."

They hadn't found any pink notes when the rooms were searched.

"Yes, he must have," Lerato said.

Spectators on the TV screen were jumping up, jubilantly celebrating something. They were South African spectators. All three women were temporarily distracted.

Judith turned up the volume. The South African batsman had hit six runs.

"Yeah!" She jubilated with the spectators in the stadium then reluctantly turned the volume down again, when she remembered that she had company.

"You seem to be quite the cricket fan. Ms Holland," Charlie said.

"Not really. In Pretoria, we prefer rugby, but I need to be able to discuss the game with my colleagues."

"Don't you play in your company's action cricket team?"

"Yes, was I supposed to say no when they asked

me to join?" She asked.

"I don't know. Maybe you should if you don't like the game that much."

"I like watching sports, not really playing them, but for the sake of the team, I can sacrifice a couple of hours during the week."

"Indeed." Lerato presented a blank page and her pen to Judith. "Could you please write down exactly, what you wrote on the note for him? Here on my pad."

"Sure." The accountant wrote down a list of figures and 'this is what I wrote' above it. She seemed satisfied with the result.

"Thank you, we'll have it checked out."

"Checked out?"

"Yes, by your boss. He'll be able to verify that the manager of the legal department needed the figures from you."

"Wynand has nothing to do with this. Most of the time he doesn't even know his arm from his elbow. It was something Julius Mandel wanted directly from me. He usually dealt with Hannah, but I needed to deal with some of those things."

"That's a bit of a harsh judgement, isn't it?"

"Well, speak to him if you must. But I'd like to get back to my cricket match now if you don't mind."

"Just one more question. How does John Bhengu fit into the picture? From your point of view."

"John Bhengu?" Her eyes were glued to the screen.

"Yes, the second victim. The receptionist. He was discovered when you returned from action cricket practise."

"Didn't you ask this before?"

"Yes, we questioned everybody, who was there, but you are an accountant and familiar with sequences. How does a receptionist fit in with an accountant and the manager of the financial department?"

"Oh, I don't know. Maybe he saw something he shouldn't have?" Judith Holland answered. "I really can't say."

"Quite possibly. Thank you for answering our questions," Lerato said in conclusion. There was nothing else she could ask.

"That's okay. You're just doing your job. We are all just doing our job…"

"Indeed, we are." Lerato got up from the couch

and Charlie did too. "We'll see ourselves out, then."

"Yes, goodbye." Judith Holland didn't pay much attention to her visitors anymore.

She was eating chips from a bowl she was holding on her knees, engrossed in the cricket match and they heard her turn up the volume of the cricket game again as Lerato closed the door behind them with a thud.

*

"So she thinks she might be psychic," Lerato said in a mocking tone.

"I'm not an expert, so I can't be sure that it's true. Maybe it's different for everyone. Not a bad story, but shouldn't a polygraph test pick up if someone dreamed something like that or if she actually saw it – or even did it herself."

"Are you saying she might have seen the body and simply pushed it out of her mind because it was so frightening for her?"

"If that's true, anybody in the company would be getting nightmares and fail the test. Why did only Judith Holland and the security guard show deception in the test results?"

"Perhaps her mind is trying to protect her. She may have witnessed something and can't talk about it. I mean she seemed rather detached from it all. That's gonna be a tough one to crack." Lerato shook her head. "What do you think? Is it possible that she made it all up?"

"I'm not a psychologist, but anything is possible. I mean I dream about stuff like that and have never been involved in a murder or been tested by a polygrapher."

"What if she just uses it as an excuse?"

"I saw white vapour behind her." Charlie finally told Lerato.

"Again? At last, you're picking up something this time. What do you think it could mean? Was it the lawyer?"

"If I just knew. There must be something she's hiding from us. The vapour started swirling around when she said that she can't recall anything unusual when she went to Hannah Bradlow's apartment."

Charlie put her seatbelt on. They heard more jubilation as they left the complex.

No doubt, everybody was watching the cricket

game.

"So she must have seen or heard something and is just too scared to talk about it," Lerato stated. "Or she knows the person she saw or heard and that's why she doesn't want to tell us. Can't you try and summon the ghost of one of the victims."

"That's not how it works," Charlie said. "They must want to come to me. I can try to speak to them, but there is no guarantee that a ghost will show up. I tried in her apartment just now, but nothing happened."

"So something is holding them back?" Lerato asked.

"Maybe. It might still happen. Remember, it took the professor's ghost a while to show himself to me."

"Yeah, and then he didn't want to go away." Lerato was referring to Professor Gerald Morton, a zoologist, who had been bludgeoned to death in the Kruger Park while studying the denning habits of wild dogs. The second case they had solved together and that had landed Lerato in a dangerous situation.

"Well, he helped us quite a bit in solving the case," Charlie reminded her friend.

"Yes, he did. I'm just saying."

They drove back to the Maitirelo office in Parktown North and Lerato phoned Inspector Johan Phaladi, who had been paying a visit to the other MultoPharm employee, who had failed the polygraph test.

"Johan isn't answering his phone," She said to Charlie.

"Do you think he's still busy with the interview?"

"We did two interviews and are finished by now, so I assume that he must be finished as well."

"He went with a colleague. Maybe they've stopped for a bite to eat."

"Could be. Let me call him again."

His phone rang and rang, but Johan Phaladi didn't answer his phone even this time around.

Chapter EIGHT

Lerato dialled again and eventually, a man answered. 'Hello, this is Robert.'

'Robert? I thought this was Johan Phaladi's phone.' Lerato replied obviously confused. Charlie looked at her, pulling a quizzical face. *Who is Robert,* she thought.

'It is.' The man said without explaining why he had answered the detective's phone. There was an uncomfortable pause.

'This is Lerato Gwala. I work with Johan. And who are you, Robert?'

There was a chance that Johan's phone had been stolen and this Robert-person was the thief. If so, she would find out.

'Oh, you are the PI lady? I'm Sergeant Robert Mangwe. We had an accident on the way back. Johan had a shock and hurt his nose.'

'OMG, you had an accident? Is he badly injured?' Lerato felt dread creeping up.

'Don't know yet. The paramedics are busy with him. Probably not broken, but they want to make sure.'

Sergeant Mangwe spoke to somebody and had a short conversation with that person. Presumably a paramedic.

'Hello? What happened?' Lerato sounded seriously worried now. Charlie sat up to listen more closely.

'Hello… sorry. Somebody jumped a red traffic light just outside of Vosloorus and caught us in the front,' Robert explained. 'Bashed our bumper. Johan had his seatbelt on, but the airbag hit him in the face. The idiot driver's drunk and in a lot of trouble now. Local police are processing the accident. Wasn't easy to get them out here with the cricket game in full swing. Our car is being towed back to Joburg. We are just waiting for a lift from a colleague.'

'Lucky, Johan had you with him. Who is picking you guys up?' Lerato jumped up.

'Somebody from the department. There are no patrol cars in the area. Karen van der Merwe said she'd come, but she's still at some family thing in Pretoria.'

'Before I forget, Robert, you spoke to the security

guard Herbert Tuins, didn't you?' Lerato asked the sergeant.

'Yes, yes we did. As much as his busy children allowed us to speak.'

'And what did he say?'

'The man was rattled by the test results. He couldn't explain why the polygraph had tested him as deceptive. He was on the top floor, looking into a broken lock when his colleague downstairs alerted him. He was becoming friends with the receptionist and he was truly sad that he would be no longer around. We had the impression that he was telling the truth.'

'I see. Thank you. We'll speak to Johan as soon as he's feeling better. You should call Karen and tell her that somebody else is coming. We can give you guys a ride. Where exactly are you?'

Sergeant Robert Mangwe gave Lerato the directions and immediately phoned Karen van der Merwe to let her know that she was off the hook.

She sounded relieved that she didn't have to leave her uncle's anniversary party early. 'You sure you'll be okay?' Her question was more dutiful than caring.

Robert Mangwe was not her favourite colleague.

Although friendly, he still treated her like an outsider and he was not the only one.

Marius Vorster and Johan Phaladi were much easier to work with. Of course, she cared about her colleagues' wellbeing, but it was better if the two private investigators were picking them up.

'Yes, I think they are already on their way,' Robert Mangwe answered.

He was keen to leave the scene of the accident as quickly as possible. In any case, he was not too fond of women in the homicide department. They could be distracting at the best of times.

'Well, in that case,' Inspector van der Merwe said. 'I hope Johan will be okay. Blasted thing to happen to you guys.' She said and took another sip of the Gin & Tonic she was holding.

'I'm alright. Johan's nose is not broken, just bleeding and he had a shock, but he'll live,' the police sergeant told her.

'Good, good, under the circumstances. Hope he recovers quickly. Then we'll see you guys at work tomorrow.'

Her aunt was calling her and Karen went back

outside to join the rest of the family for the celebrations on the veranda.

*

On Monday morning, the polygraph test was already set up in one of the small windowless offices on the second floor.

"… and then I'll ask you if you had anything to do with either of the murders."

The polygrapher went through the steps of preparing the first subject for the test, while his second subject waited outside in the passage.

It would have been against the rules not to tell Judith Holland what to expect during the test. This didn't have any influence on the outcome, but the rules dictated this approach.

Lerato had asked him about Judith's alleged psychic disposition, but he hadn't been sure about it. In all the years he'd been conducting these tests, it was the first time, the question of a subject being psychic had cropped up.

"Why are you telling me all of this again?" Judith asked him. "You told me the same thing the other time you were here."

The man had brought his equipment and set everything up on the only desk in the windowless room. She had listened to her guided meditation in the car, but she was still nervous about the test.

This could mess up her career prospects if she wasn't careful, but then it wasn't just her career that bothered her.

"It's procedure. We have to give the questions I'll ask during the pre-test interview so the test subject won't be surprised, which might give us a false reading," he sighed, but explained patiently. If he was paid a Rand every time he had to answer this question…

"Yes, you said so the first time around," the accountant said impatiently. "But then there was something wrong with the test anyway, I'm sure. Can we get on with it? I still have a mountain of work waiting for me on my desk."

The polygrapher applied the clamps to her fingertips and checked that the device was in order. "We will find out in a minute. It's different to what you are used to seeing in the movies… ready when you are." He went down his list of questions.

"Is your name Judith Holland?"

"Yes." The lines on the paper remained smooth.

"Do you work for the company MultoPharm?"

"Yes."

"Are you married?" The question was as monotone as the previous ones, but there was some reaction from the subject and the lines were slightly curvy.

"No."

The easy questions came first before he got to the questions that had to do with the murder cases.

He had been informed that one of the managers had been killed during the company's Christmas party, so there were three murders to be investigated now. He had updated the questions accordingly.

They had decided that nobody else should be in the room with him and the test subject this time, so Charlie and Lerato were sitting in one of the adjoining rooms, waiting for the results of the test.

Johan had phoned earlier to say that he would come with Karen van der Merwe.

Since the double date with Marius Vorster and her brother Jono, Karen had not been exactly Charlie's favourite person. Now, the brusque blonde was partnering with Johan Phaladi and would be involved in the MultoPharm murder cases. No matter, this was work and she would be professional about it.

Meanwhile, the polygrapher continued with his questions in the other room.

"Do you hold a grudge against Hannah Bradlow or any of your other colleagues?" He asked Judith Holland.

"No, not really, except for the occasional work-related quibble, you know."

The needles on the broad paper strip drew wild elongated curves, quite different to the rather smooth lines up till now. Judith Holland couldn't see what the needle was doing, but she would be damned if she told him how

Hannah had asked her to assess the value of patents then forced her to inflate their value.

To Judith's mind, this was just wrong, not to mention illegal. Then she was asked to record a number of transactions wrongly. When she questioned this, Hannah had been rather snide about it and told her to do as she was told.

Obviously, Judith couldn't disclose this now,

because it might be construed as a motive if they had it in for her. She had seen enough crime stories on TV to know how these things were linked up.

Apart from the fact that she'd be in hell's kitchen for talking about such company matters, if they needed a suspect… well let's say she's on top of the list.

In her mind's eye, Judith saw the slumped over body of Hannah Bradlow on the lawn behind the apartment building.

Luckily, she hadn't handed her the documents yet. They were still at home in her apartment.

"Sorry?" She seemed to wake up from a daydream. The polygrapher had asked her another question.

"I asked you if you know anything about John Bhengu's death."

"No," she said and the needles drew wild lines all over the paper.

"How well did you know John Bhengu?"

"Not very well. I had only just started working at MultoPharm when all of this happened." The lines flattened out.

"Did you have anything to do with Julius Mandel's death?"

"No." The needles of the polygraph went wild again. Judith had a secret. A dirty secret by any standards. In order to pay for her studies, she had occasionally moonlighted as a call girl.

And back in the day, Julius Mandel had been one of her customers.

*

"So, you are feeling better today?" Lerato asked Johan Phaladi two rooms down the passage. He and Inspector van der Merwe had just arrived at the company. Some other case had held them up at the office downtown. They were waiting for the polygrapher to give them the results for Judith Holland and Herbert Tuins and Karen van der Merwe was working on her laptop.

"Yes, I told you. It was just a scratch." He pointed to his nose, which was covered by a plaster. "I took two Panados and went to bed last night. This morning I felt okay."

"A true man," Lerato grinned at them. "As long as you didn't have whiplash or something. What about Robert?"

"Well, you saw him yesterday. Not a scratch on

him and he's working on another case today. Thanks, by the way, for partnering with me today, Karen," the inspector turned to his colleague.

"No sweat," the tough policewoman looked up briefly. "I hope we can solve this case – or better even all three cases – soon. There could be a serial killer afoot. Imagine that." She went back to writing her report.

"Let's hope not," Inspector Phaladi sighed.

"The polygraph test should give us some indication of that. Although it's weird that a straight-arrow like Judith Holland could have been found to be deceptive." Lerato looked at Charlie, who seemed mesmerised by a spot on the wall. "Charlie?"

Was her friend sad again? But this time, Charlie responded immediately.

"Can I speak to you outside, Lerato?" She asked.

"Sure, when?"

"Now would be good." Charlie gestured with her head toward the door.

"Well then …excuse us for a moment." Lerato nodded to the police inspectors and followed Charlie into the passage.

"You can leave the door open," Karen van der Merwe said. "I need some air. It's so stuffy in here."

She went back to working on her report and Johan opened his jacket to make himself more comfortable.

"Sure," Lerato said and Charlie walked away from the open door and stopped on the other side of the passage to have a word with her friend in private.

"What's up?" Lerato wanted to know. "Any messages from… the other side?"

"Sort of. How should I put it?" Charlie began.

"What? It's about time, too," Lerato said. "So?"

"The lawyer doesn't seem to like Karen very much," Charlie explained.

"What lawyer?"

"The one, who died during the Christmas party."

Lerato was stunned. "Really? Why? Did he follow us out here?"

"Yes," Charlie replied simply. "To be honest, I don't like Karen very much either, but the lawyer seems to have a grudge against her."

"No way. Does he have anything to say about how he was killed? I mean Karen wasn't even there…" Lerato asked.

"She didn't kill him, silly. He just seemed upset about Karen somehow and obviously, he didn't want to engage with me in there. He kept signalling at the door."

She pointed to the room they'd just left. "So that's why we're out here."

"Where is he?"

"I can't see him now." Charlie turned around.

"Alright, we're out here, waiting for your ghost. He sure is moody, but ask him to be more specific. We know that Karen didn't kill him. I mean that would be weird anyway, she's a policewoman." Lerato shrugged her shoulders. "So what does he want?"

"Wait, he's here." Charlie concentrated for a while. "He shows me images. Seems he was arrested at a bar in Pretoria a few years ago," she finally said. "I can see a dominatrix doing some sort of show between the tables. Apparently, he knew Judith back then as well… and Karen was one of the police officers, who arrested him. It was a seedy bar in Sunnyside. He's not very happy about the fact. He shows me how Judith got away through some backdoor. He doesn't really talk – he shows me pictures…"

"No way! Our straight-laced accountant was hanging out in fish bars in Sunnyside? What was she doing there? Maybe one of the questions the polygrapher asked her came too close to the truth and she didn't want it to be known. That's what may have caused the test result."

"Could be…" Charlie still seemed to be listening.

"So that explains why he doesn't like Karen, but what about out Judith Holland?"

"He doesn't say, but I assume that's what it was all about. She looks quite young and wears sexy clothes. Making eyes at the men in the bar."

"Picking up men as a student? Dang! That could be the motive - if he tried to blackmail her that is." Lerato felt that she was onto something.

"Hypothetically, of course." Charlie stared at the same spot in the middle of the passage.

"The lawyer's gone now, but I guess that there was something like that going on."

"Well, push me down with a feather. Maybe that's how she financed her studies. We already know that she doesn't come from a wealthy background."

Charlie nodded. "That's probably it. I'm sorry for young girls, who don't have money to go to school. Bright but poor. Look how far she's come as an accountant. And she didn't have the money and probably prostituted herself."

"That's what we assume. We still don't know that whole truth, but maybe it would be a good idea to tell the polygrapher to ask her certain questions about it," Lerato said. "It could be crucial to our case."

"Wouldn't he have to start all over, then?"

"I'm not sure how it works, but let's find out."

Lerato turned around and they walked over to the room where the polygraph test was being conducted. It was just a few meters from where they had been standing.

"Where is the other candidate?" Charlie wondered.

"Herbert Tuins, the security guard?" Lerato asked.

"Yes, him. Wasn't he supposed to be waiting out here in the passage?"

There were two chairs on the other side of the passage, but nobody was sitting on them. Nobody was in the passage at all.

"Maybe he's inside and Judith Holland's finished and went back to her office. I know we said they should wait for us, so we could discuss the results, but you never know, something urgent could have come up at work," Lerato surmised.

"Beats me. He greeted us this morning and then he sat down. He must be somewhere…" Charlie shrugged.

"Didn't you see him leave just now? You were facing in that direction."

They looked up and down the passage and saw other people walking around at the far end, but no sign of Judith Holland or the security guard.

The employees had obviously been told to stay away from the area and not to disturb the polygraph proceedings.

"To be honest, I wasn't paying attention," Charlie admitted. "The lawyer showed me all those images and I didn't notice anyone else around."

"We can find out right now. Let's go and see how the test is progressing in there."

"We should be quiet," Charlie whispered.

They listened at the door and heard a strange

muffled noise. They looked at each other. That was odd!

As soon as Lerato opened the door to the room with the polygraph machine, they stopped in their tracks.

Chapter NINE

Inside the small room, a picture of sheer chaos presented itself. Not at all what they had expected to see.

The polygrapher was sitting crookedly on a chair with his hands behind his back and his feet tied with cables.

Something was stuck in his mouth and secured with duct tape, which had prevented him from alerting anyone nearby. A cell phone lay crushed on the carpeted floor.

As soon as he'd spotted the two PIs, his eyes were about to pop out of their sockets with a desperate, pleading expression.

He grunted helplessly and tried to move the chair toward them. This was the sound they had heard through the closed door. It took Lerato only a second to take in the scene before them then she jumped into action.

She untied the man and proceeded to take the gag

out of his mouth.

"Hold still!" She ordered him.

The man flinched and grunted as she ripped the duct tape off his mouth. Lucky for him, he was cleanly shaven. He spat out the gag and took a deep breath. "She… she…" he croaked in a hoarse voice. "Didn't you hear me? I tried to call for help."

"No, sorry Jacques. We heard nothing. Do you mean Ms Holland? The subject you were testing? What did she do?"

Charlie and Lerato exchanged a puzzled look. The placid accountant was supposed to be responsible for all this?

"She threatened me with a knife!" Jacques, the polygrapher, complained.

"What? With a knife?" Lerato couldn't believe her ears. "Are you okay? Did she hurt you?"

Instead of answering he said grumpily, "I thought you had a policeman stationed outside to make sure nothing like this could happen, but obviously not. Great!"

Jacques had a good point.

"No, the inspectors are sitting in the room where

we were waiting for your test results. They are a little short-staffed, I think, and one of the inspectors got injured… and nobody expected that this would happen."

"Great," he repeated in a disappointed tone. "Two inspectors and they are hiding in another room, while I'm being threatened by this… this woman. She suddenly turned into a fury and told me to shut up. *Shut up, shut up!* She yelled at me. The test was off the charts. I tried to get to the door, but she told me to sit in the chair. Then she tied my hands and feet with the cables. Cut the cables with that knife. Now I have to replace them."

"I'm so sorry, Jacques. That shouldn't have happened," Lerato apologised.

"No, it shouldn't. I'm telling you she's dangerous! You can't let her get away." The polygrapher rubbed his wrists, while he watched Lerato untie his ankles. "She suddenly went berserk, ripped the clamps off her fingers and did this…" He pointed to himself and repeated with a shudder.

"She has that knife on her...then she slashed the cables and left with most of them. As if she had planned it all. "

"So, she's armed and dangerous."

"Bloody hell. It's her. I'm telling you she's murdered all these people," he said.

"Did she say anything to you?" Lerato asked.

"Just that she'd had enough. The polygraph went wild when she answered the questions. I can't believe you didn't station somebody outside this damn room!"

"Jacques, what did she say? Did she give you a hint where she might be heading? The security guard you were supposed to test next isn't outside."

"She didn't say anything about that, but she was furious. I was just glad when she left the room. Mumbled something about paying for something for the rest of her life. But not her…"

"If she's really the killer, you're lucky she didn't stick the knife into you."

The polygrapher closed his eyes and his mouth trembled. "I know," he whispered.

"She must have taken the security guard with her or he's her accomplice," Jacques stammered and looked over his polygraph device. "Here, look at that." He held up the paper strip that must have been generated during Judith Holland's test. The wavy lines were virtually touching each side of the strip.

"There's no doubt about it. Deception if I ever saw it." "Psychic, my foot!" He rolled his eyes and scoffed.

"That's what we came in here for. An anonymous source told us that she may have had a motive, at least when it comes to the murder of Mr. Mandel. They seemed to have known each other when she was a student and she... possibly prostituted herself. I wanted to ask you to add a few questions. That's why we came into the room."

Jacques shrugged his shoulders. "Well, it's too late now."

"We have to get a search party going," Charlie said, "... and fast. If she has a weapon, there's no telling what harm she could do."

"Johan and Karen can organise that." Lerato turned to leave. "If Mr. Tuins is her hostage, we need to find them quickly before she goes off her rocker again."

"Then you better hurry," the man said. "I have no

desire to run into that madwoman again."

He sat down and began to sort through what was left of his cables. The paper strip was still intact.

As Charlie and Lerato walked into the passage, the two police officers were already coming toward them. "What's going on? You were taking forever out here, so we thought we should come and check. Did something happen?"

"You can say that!" Charlie declared.

"Judith Holland failed the test again and blew a fuse," Lerato told them. "Apparently threatened our polygrapher with a knife, gagged him and tied him to a chair. He's inside and not very happy. We need reinforcements to search the premises before she puts anybody else in danger."

"Good grief!" Karen van der Merwe didn't know what to say. "Judith Holland?" She was holding a backpack with her laptop inside. At least she'd finished the report.

"Took the security guard with her and a bunch of cables," Lerato explained.

"We should have waited outside with the man," Karen said. "Damn!"

Lerato checked on the polygrapher. "Jacques is alright, just a bit shaken. Lucky she didn't hurt him."

"Nobody could have predicted that," Charlie said.

"Still…" Karen van der Merwe sighed unhappily. "Where could she have gone, though?"

Johan Phaladi was already talking to someone on his mobile phone in an urgent voice. "Yes, send everybody you can. God knows what she's up to. I know, I know, but she has a weapon… a knife. Right now would be good. Okay, yes, at MultoPharm in Kramerville. Just google it, man. Okay, we'll see you now."

"And?" Karen asked him.

"Marius is dropping everything to come here with a gang of officers."

"No pun intended?" Charlie asked, then realised that this was not the time for joking remarks.

"What?" Johan Phaladi stared at her.

"Never mind, Johan. Shouldn't we get a head start? It's likely that they are still in the building," Lerato said in an urgent voice.

"The woman is quite dangerous and we know what she's capable of, but we also have weapons." Karen touched the gun in her holster.

"Well then. Where do we start?" Ex-policewoman Lerato asked impatiently.

"This floor."

"Are you sure? Shouldn't we rather split up?" Inspector Phaladi asked.

"There are only three of us."

"Four," Charlie piped up.

"Okay four then," Karen said. "Can you handle a weapon?"

"No, but I could if you show me how…"

The police inspector rolled her eyes. "Three then."

"Charlie will be helpful in locating the two of them," Lerato said. "It's one of her specialities."

"Oh really? What, is she like telepathic or something?"

Lerato gave her an affirming look.

"No way. You can't be serious. You believe in that kind of crap?" Karen sneered.

Charlie looked offended.

"It's not crap," Lerato said in her friend's defence. "She's helped us with other cases."

"Let's go. We are losing too much time." Karen

van der Merwe jumped into action.

"Do you all want to stand around and chat or are we going to look for the perp?" Inspector Phaladi asked impatiently.

"The policewoman pointed to the left. "You guys start on the other side. Any objections or should I ask you where they are?" She gave Charlie a mocking glance.

"I can feel some hot anger coming from all around right now," Charlie answered unperturbed.

"Oh, I see. Some help you are," the female inspector said. "And you do what you must do."

"Stop it already," Lerato said in a heated tone that Karen was not used to. "I told you, she's helped solve other difficult cases…"

Karen realised that she was overstepping a line.

"I better put this into the car." She pointed to her laptop and walked down the stairs, taking two steps at a time.

Johan Phaladi rolled his eyes in a silent apology. "You alright?"

Lerato nodded. "Okay then, let's start over there." He pointed to the left. "Are your phones on?"

"Yes," Charlie looked at her phone.

"Then let's go."

*

Inspector Vorster arrived surprisingly fast and soon with the reinforcement of half a dozen police officers.

They were searching the company garden and were combing the area from the parking lot all the way to the palisade fence and the lawns and flowerbeds at the back. Then they moved into the ground floor of the building, where they continued their search. Staff members had been quietly evacuated and waited outside the reception.

By then, Lerato and Charlie were searching the third floor and Karen and Johan the second floor, while Marius Vorster was at the reception and requested to see today's video recordings.

"Do you think, Herbert will be alright? I mean, he has a wife and two kids," the anxious secretary, who stood in as the receptionist today, asked him.

"Who?" Inspector Vorster was distracted as he fast-forwarded through this morning's video.

"The security guard, who's with Ms. Holland," the

secretary said.

"Oh, I see. I certainly hope so," he answered.

A check of the video recordings had revealed that Judith Holland and the other suspect had not left the building, at least not through the normal entranceways.

So it was likely that they were still inside the building. He informed the sergeant in charge of the search on the first floor and the company gardens.

Video cameras on the other floors were not functional. Since the murder of the male receptionist, the tapes had not been updated and a few cameras had been out of order for a while.

"Darn!" Marius Vorster was disappointed.

This could drag their search out, and who knew what condition they would find the two escapees in. Plus, Charlie was somewhere in the building and he didn't know where.

Neither Charlie nor Lerato were answering their phones, which made him nervous.

"I'm sorry, inspector," the secretary apologised. "We haven't had a chance to interview a new receptionist before Christmas. Management wanted to wait until January to employ someone to train, so it's been just secretaries taking turns. There was just no time…"

Meanwhile, oblivious to what was going on at the reception, Lerato and Charlie were searching the third floor, where only one policewoman was stationed between the stairs and the elevator to keep an eye on things.

They had a master key, but so far, all the doors they had checked were open and no sign of Judith Holland or Herbert Tuins.

As they were about to walk past the finance department, Charlie felt a nudge and saw movement through the security glass window. A second take confirmed that somebody was inside the office.

She tapped Lerato's arm and indicated that she had seen something. The two PIs took a step back, leaning against the wall to the right of the door and whispered in hushed voices.

"What did you see?"

"I'm pretty sure it's them." Charlie pointed to the door.

"Both of them?" Lerato mouthed.

"I didn't see," Charlie murmured and shrugged.

"But all the accountants are downstairs or should be."

"Okay, here's what we'll do..." Lerato explained her plan to Charlie, who nodded silently. Then she dialled Johan Phaladi's number. The policewoman by the elevator didn't look their way and although Lerato waved, the officer didn't react.

So she took a wide berth around the office to speak to the woman and motioned for Charlie to stay where she was.

Charlie waited next to the door leaning against the wall when she saw the spectre of the lawyer slowly appear in front of her again.

Earlier, he had shown her what had happened during the police raid on a nightclub in Pretoria and that Judith Holland had been there, too. Charlie was hopeful that he was prepared to help her with this new situation.

The spectre was hovering in front of the door and moved his head to indicate that she should move away from it a little more. Charlie complied.

Lerato discussed something with the policewoman in hushed tones and lifted her cell phone to her ear. She turned around briefly to face Charlie before turning her back again.

The apparition didn't do much apart from hovering in front of Charlie. There was no way that anybody, who was inside the Finance office could see him through the glass window, but she couldn't be sure. Why didn't he do anything or show her something that might help with the investigations?

"What should we do?" She asked the deceased man, but still nothing.

Why did John Bhengu and Hannah Bradlow remain so elusive, now that she needed them?

They hadn't shown up at all or communicated, apart from possibly generating the vapour that surrounded Judith Holland at the Christmas party and at her apartment, while Lerato had questioned her.

Finally, the spectre communicated and his answer astonished her. Not that he spoke or anything, but he indicated to Charlie that Lerato's plan – whatever it was - needed to be changed. Urgently.

"Lerato…" Charlie called softly.

Lerato Gwala looked in her direction, shook her head and gestured for Charlie to stop talking. She kept pressing the phone to her ear and nodded, while the policewoman looked on.

"Listen…" Charlie insisted and waved again. "You must change something."

'Excuse me a moment, Johan,' Lerato whispered into the phone, held her hand over it before turning to Charlie. "What is it?" She whispered. They could barely hear each other across the distance.

"The lawyer says you shouldn't do it that way," Charlie said almost imperceptively.

"What lawyer?" Lerato creased her face and shook her head.

"You know… Mandel… Julius Mandel… the guy who got killed at the Christmas party… he's over there…" Charlie pointed with her chin to where she was seeing the spectre. "He says you shouldn't try to break into the office from the balcony. The two of us should enter through the door and …" The ghostly lawyer nodded in agreement. Of course, nobody but Charlie could see him, but Lerato knew better than to ignore Charlie's suggestion.

"Change of plan." She spoke into the phone in a low voice, while nodding to the policewoman. "We are going in from the passage."

A proper plan was beginning to take shape, but Charlie felt uneasy all the same standing on her own so close to a killer.

Chapter TEN

Charlie watched the spectre of Julius Mandel slowly fade away. *No*, she thought with intent, *don't go away just yet*. The spectre didn't seem to care and soon there was nothing more to see but thin air.

Well then, she would have to do without his help. Perhaps it would be a good idea to join Lerato and the policewoman by the stairs… but she was standing on the other side of the door.

Even if she ducked past the security glass window, it was possible that Judith Holland might get a glimpse of her.

At the far end of the passage, two men hurried down the stairs. How they had dodged the evacuation of the building, Charlie didn't know. She couldn't worry about details like that. She decided to simply stay out of sight for now and wait.

There was a sudden commotion inside the finance office.

The noises she heard didn't promise anything

good, but Charlie didn't dare look at what was going on. It sounded like moaning and punching as far as she could tell. She could sense that the situation was worsening.

Charlie took a deep breath and closed her eyes. All she could do was wait and hope that they wouldn't find another dead body at the end of the day.

Charlie felt increasingly uncomfortable. What was taking Lerato so long? Should she just take a chance and duck past the door?

What was the worst that could happen? Judith Holland was already off her rocker.

It was clear that the accountant had killed before and not just once. The polygraph test had kicked off an unfortunate series of events and there was no telling what might set her volatile temper off again. The mere thought made Charlie feel like running for the hills.

She wanted Lerato to hurry up, but her friend still stood in front of the staircase with her back turned, explaining something to the policewoman and Charlie didn't want to draw unnecessary attention to herself. What were they still talking about?

It felt like an eternity to her.

The policewoman seemed to have trouble understanding what Lerato was saying, but then she began to nod slowly. Good, their discussion was coming to an end. It wouldn't take much longer now.

Charlie sent Lerato a hurried message and saw her reading it. Maybe better speak to her directly. She dialled Lerato's number.

As her friend turned around, the door next to Charlie opened. This took her by surprise and she didn't put up a fight when a hand grabbed her arm roughly and dragged her inside in a flash. She felt pain shooting up her arm.

"What… what…" she stammered then yelled, "Lerato, Lerato!" She felt fear and anger at the same time. Charlie was angry at the spectre because the lawyer was supposed to help her and he had just faded away.

He had made her understand that things would improve if the police changed their plan and now this was happening!

She managed to let the phone slide into her pocket just in time and tried to stop the door with her foot from closing, but her foot slid inside as she was dragged with surprising force and fell against a nearby desk, knocking over the computer monitor.

Charlie lost her balance but managed to hold onto the desk.

Slap, slap. She felt sharp, hot pain on her face that matched the pain on her back and her arm.

"Ouch! What are you doing…"

"Shut up, bitch." It was Judith Holland's voice. Cold and demanding and so unlike the placid accountant she remembered from the interviews and the Christmas party, but it was definitely her.

"Pick that up and put it back! We do important work here." The voice ordered.

Charlie thought for a split second that she should just pull away and run toward the door as quick as she could, but a glance at the door confirmed that there was no chance of escape.

She was simply in the weaker position and battling a deranged woman, who pointed a bloodied knife at her face, was out of the question.

Blood? Had she killed the security guard or somebody else? Charlie shivered but bent down obediently and picked up the monitor.

"Did you really think I didn't know you were standing out there spying on me?" Charlie instinctively knew that she wouldn't be able to convince Judith that what she was doing was wrong and should surrender to the police. At least not now.

Her instinct told her that what she needed to do was think on her feet and calm the accountant down somehow. *Think*, she reminded herself, *think*.

With some luck, she would receive a helping hand anytime now from somebody, who was invisible to the other woman or the police would execute their new plan.

If she just knew what that plan was.

She closed her eyes and thought intently. *Where are you?* The spectre of Julius Mandel was still elusive, but Charlie was sure that he could hear her plea, and so could the others who were hovering in the vicinity.

She promptly thought of another way to communicate with Lerato. The phone was still in her pocket! It was important not to lose her connection to the world outside this office.

"Who are you?" she asked. "What do you want from me?"

She acted as if she didn't know who had dragged her into the office. Perhaps this would create some doubt in the woman's mind. Charlie carefully put the monitor back and leaned against the desk.

She still hadn't spotted Herbert Tuins, the security guard, and was afraid that she might see a dead body.

"What do you mean 'who are you'? Haven't you figured that one out yet?" Judith snapped and drew her face an ugly grimace. "Miss Private Detective…"

"Ms Holland?" Charlie asked, pleading innocence. "But I thought you were downstairs."

"Yes, it's me. Who else?" The woman interrupted her rudely. "Pah, downstairs!"

Somebody groaned in the front and Charlie's eyes darted over to the wall with the whiteboard, where the sound was coming from.

That's when she saw the security guard kneeling with his back against the wall. His face looked bloodied and his hands and feet were tied together behind his back. Duct tape covered his mouth.

Charlie felt pity for the man. That was not a good

situation, but on the other hand, he was still alive. He was slightly built and apparently no match for the heftier accountant. How she had managed to get him to come with her to the finance office was unclear. By fluke, nobody had been around.

The only way was that Judith Holland might have forced him to come with her was up the back stairs, the duct tape already covering his mouth, hiding until everybody had left. It didn't matter right now.

Charlie drew her glance away from the man's pleading eyes. As sorry as she felt for him, she couldn't afford to lose her cool now.

Every ounce of her attention was trained on how to get them safely out of the room and the woman's grasp. She would do whatever was necessary.

Judith Holland noticed Charlie's gaze. She turned around to the bedraggled man. "What did I tell you? Shut the f*** up! This is all your fault."

The woman took a couple of steps toward him and raised her hand before getting a hold of herself when Charlie cried, "Don't hurt him! Please…"

She was shocked at the foul language the accountant was using and at her ugly demeanour. The woman had seemed more refined before. Now she was just a foul-mouthed shrew. A ruthless killer.

Charlie couldn't think of a psychological condition that described what she was witnessing, but clearly, she was beyond deranged. Maybe hiding her double life all these years had pushed her over the edge?

"What is it with you people? Why do you have to talk all the time? My head hurts from all that chatter!" The accountant pressed her hands against her temples in a helpless gesture and Charlie spoke up.

"What do you expect, if you treat me like this? Must I just silently accept being pushed around? You barely know me." Charlie's rare Greek temper made a short-lived appearance.

"You better just accept it if you want to live a while longer," Judith Holland growled.

The words felt like punches to the stomach and Charlie saw the knife pointing at her again. The accountant wasn't joking. The knife came dangerously close to her face and Judith's eyes became narrow slits. "You want some of this?"

Charlie knew that she only had a chance when she kept a cool head. For her own sake and that of the hapless security guard. Lerato and the police would somehow figure out what to do to get them to safety.

"No, no of course not. Please don't point that at me," she pleaded.

Judith Holland closed her eyes tightly.

"Do you have a headache?" She asked the woman in a more caring tone.

Judith Holland seemed to relax a little. "This is all just too much! Too much for me!" She moaned. "Nobody is cutting me any slack."

Charlie noticed how a tear was sliding down her cheek. This was unexpected and showed how much pressure the accountant was under.

"What's too much?" Charlie felt that keeping the woman talking would be a good move under the circumstances.

Finally, she saw her chance. Charlie's fingers were busy, switching on the cell phone's recording function in her pocket. Amazing what you could do if you really had to. She looked down to check during a rare moment when her captor turned around to stare at the security guard. "Him for example…"

The man whimpered helplessly, but Charlie

couldn't get distracted now. For her sake and his.

Yes, it seemed that she had managed to record their conversation. She'd send it to Lerato then repeated the process. With some luck, the police would be able to hear what was being said inside the office. That's the way she could think of.

She sighed and kept an eye on the woman once again. At the very least, if she kept talking to her, it would bring down the level of tension. Hopefully.

"What?" The accountant turned around to face Charlie again. Clearly, the security guard was behaving well in his corner.

"I asked you 'what's too much?'" Charlie repeated and tried to look friendly.

"Everything. Everything!" The voice was cutting again. Judith Holland's mood seemed to change from moment to moment. "Keep your hands where I can see them!"

Charlie held her hands up to show that she didn't have a weapon.

"I'm just looking for a painkiller in my bag. I know I have some aspirin in there somewhere. Maybe that will help with your headache." It wasn't even a lie. She truly wanted the woman to feel better.

She pointed to the small bag she carried across her chest and sent the recording with the other hand. Then she pressed the recording button down again. It worked. Charlie felt better. The woman hadn't noticed her little manoeuver.

"Okay. Thanks. But slowly…" The idea of painkillers seemed attractive to the killer, who was obviously struggling with a headache.

The woman waved the knife around and Charlie kept her eyes fixed on it while trying to find the pain tablets with her hand.

They were part of the basics she always carried with her. She sighed with relief when her fingers touched the metallic wrapping of the tablets.

"Okay I found the painkillers," she gave the woman the heads-up, never averting her eyes from the knife. "I'm pulling my hand out now."

She handed the wrapped tablets to Judith who impatiently tore the aspirin from Charlie's hand and fiddled with the wrapping, while Charlie checked on the cell phone in her pocket. It was recording.

Was it safe to make a move toward the door, while

the woman was busy?

Judith Holland popped two of the tablets into her mouth and continued to point her weapon at Charlie. No, it was not safe, she decided.

"Everybody's against me," the accountant wailed, while still chewing the tablets. "Everybody. All I wanted was a chance in life. Is that too much to ask?"

Why didn't she go to the watercooler in the corner and flush them down with some water? No such luck. Charlie felt awkward being so nice to her but looked at the killer with some empathy nevertheless.

"No, that's not too much to ask."

The woman continued to speak with tears in her eyes. "I wish I had someone on my side for a change. But not even David's on my side anymore. He found another sweetheart, the cheat! Somebody has to pay for all the pain I'm in. I don't care, who is paying, but enough is enough."

Her changing moods were mind-boggling.

"Who hurt you?" Charlie asked. Her instinct telling her what to say.

"Who? You're asking me who? Everyone! I can't win - but I swear I take some of you pigs with me!"

The answer was vicious and a tear rolled down her cheek. Judith Holland wiped it away impatiently.

Charlie watched her and tried to think. She wasn't trained to communicate with people, who'd lost their marbles. Where on earth was the helping hand from the 'other side' when she needed it?

"I'm truly sorry that people were horrible to you," she said, "but not everybody is the same. Believe me, most people are not like that."

"Most people? Pah! Tell that to those a**holes, who have nothing better to do than to torture others… torture them with their hatred, their lies. Being mean and blaming me for everything. What have I done to deserve that?" She was pushing her hands against her head again. Maybe she needed more tablets? But two aspirin were all Charlie had in her bag.

"Blame you?" She asked innocently. The recording was still going.

"Yes. Hannah thought it would be a good idea to defraud the company and when things were about to come out, she wanted to blame it on me. Me! The lawyer was in on it and didn't want to listen either. 'Once a whore, always a whore…' he said. Said that to me. I did my dues. It's all in the past now and I have the certificates to prove that I worked hard. He should have left it right where it was – the past. But… he didn't. He knew what I did to get myself through university - that was the beginning of the end. Nobody would understand that I hadn't touched those documents. Didn't even know what they had done. I'm an honest person."

So, that was her motive? *An honest accountant, but a vicious killer,* Charlie thought. Keep her talking, keep her talking. "What happened then?"

"Oh, are we a therapist now?" The woman hissed, but changed her mind in mid-flight and said calmer. "Oh alright, I'll tell you…"

Charlie took a deep breath and tried to stay calm. "Please do that. It will make you feel better, I'm sure." She tried to speak in a soothing voice.

"Don't tell me what to do." The shrew spoke again and Charlie wondered if Judith Holland might be schizophrenic. Not that she knew much about this condition, but there had to be an explanation for her erratic behaviour.

"Okay then, I won't," she said slowly.

Judith seemed lost in thought for a while before she spoke again. Perhaps the painkillers were working after all.

"Hannah had cooked up this scheme with Julius Mandel…" she snorted with contempt at the thought. "I discovered the irregularities in their calculations, of course. How could I not have? I'm a good accountant and they were badly disguised. Did they think I was stupid? I didn't know it was them and told Hannah about my findings. She told me to drop the matter… I mean just drop it? Just like that? I will never be a part of fraud. Never! Thought I didn't know what I was doing and would just play along. Pah!"

Could an obvious attempt at cooking the books drive someone like Judith Holland over the edge? Maybe there was more to the story. Given her history as a prostitute, she must have been through a lot, and Julius Mandel reminding her of her past had probably not been the best idea.

"She wanted me to do her bidding and take the documents to her apartment. I thought maybe we can talk about this and she would try to do the right thing after all." Judith Holland paused for a moment. "So I went to her apartment after hours, but I was angry. Very angry. The report was already late and she wanted me to sign it off. I wanted nothing to do with the fraud. I mean just because I'm new at the company doesn't mean that I don't know how the value of assets is assessed and those patents just didn't look right to me from the start. Now I'm not so sure anymore… but those overstated assets inflated the value. I mean I understand why they were doing it… to hide the theft then make the company look better on paper and get investment and all that. But it was wrong."

Charlie tried to follow her ramblings.

She didn't know much about accounting but saw that Judith must have been very upset about the expectations Hannah Bradlow had made clear to her in a demanding manner. Expectations that had eventually cost her her life.

It was understandable how she could feel so strongly about the corruption at work and the pressure she'd been under, but cruelly killing her colleagues, instead of reporting them…

In her mind, somebody had to pay – and the

payment was still ongoing.

Had Charlie heard a sound outside? Where was her backup?

"I'm afraid I don't quite follow. What kind of assets are you talking about?" Charlie gave it a shot and her question went down surprisingly well.

"Let me explain," Judith said. "A lot of work goes into assessing the value of assets, such as patents for formulas and medicines… Hannah had done all of that before I even joined the company. Having me work on it and using the figures in the report would have looked legit to an outsider. She didn't think I would know enough about it to realise what they had done and kept pushing me to sign off the report. But I did know. Ah, whatever…" She waved the knife through the air in a gesture of frustration.

Charlie didn't understand what exactly the accountant was talking about and feared that the woman would stop talking if she didn't ask her the right questions. She had to push for more time, while this was recorded.

"That's unbelievable," Charlie agreed. "Who would not have been angry?"

Again, her instinct dictated the words that she spoke.

"You know what really made me angry?" Another tear rolled down the woman's face and suffered the same fate as the previous one.

"No, what was it?" Charlie asked.

"The way Julius Mandel talked to me during the last zoom meeting. He barked insults at me. Dropped the f-bomb I don't know how many times. The way he would treat a prostitute, no doubt. I mean he swore at me. So disrespectful…"

"What a prick…" Charlie agreed.

She saw the colour in one corner of the room change to red. Was it the lawyer, Julius Mandel? She should watch what she was saying or the spectre would not want to help her at all. "That's unbelievable."

Should she send the recording off or wait? Lerato was surely expecting more recordings to come through, but Charlie decided to wait a while longer.

Judith Holland was practically confessing what she had done and why.

"He had the audacity to demand a session with me

during the Christmas party. If you know what I mean. Said he'd tell management about my past and that he knew what I'd done to Hannah Bradlow and the receptionist…"

"John Bhengu?"

"Yes, yes… that one. Julius said he knew, what I'd done," she repeated in an irritated tone. "So he demanded sex outside by the generator. He knew nobody would be there during the party. Especially not when it was raining cats and dogs."

"That's unbelievable! What a pig." Charlie was truly outraged. The red colour was getting more intense in the corner of the room.

"You see! That's what I thought… He wanted to blackmail me on top of things."

The man by the wall tried to ease the pain in his wrists and ankles as noiselessly as possible. Charlie saw his endeavours from the corner of her eye, while she stayed focused on the woman standing in front of her. Surely, the police had devised a strategy to get the murderous accountant under control.

"Do you mind if I sit down?" Charlie asked.

"Sure." The woman replied with a sloppy gesture

toward a nearby chair and Charlie felt a little bit more comfortable sitting than standing against the desk. As far as this was possible when someone pointed a knife at you and became angry at the slightest provocation.

"So tell me how this happened. I'd say you were provoked."

"Yes… yes, I was," she said. "Hannah spoke to me as if it was her right to order me around, but it's just not right to defraud people. We are supposed to do clean audits, to show good character and she threatened me. Told me that Mr. Mandel had told her about what… what I had done in the past. I swear I needed to survive, needed to pay for food and the room and study fees. And my books weren't cheap."

Judith Holland didn't answer Charlie's question, but she went along with it.

"It's expensive to study."

"Yes, it is and my mother had no money to give me. 'Why don't you get a job at SARS or in sales?' she would ask me, but I wanted more. I wanted to make more money and be happy. Find a good husband and have a family. Not just work to survive. I want to travel, own a house. Is that too much to ask?

So I did what I have to do. And they tried to turn it around against me! One more person, who knew about me. I just couldn't let them destroy me. I didn't have a choice."

"I see." Charlie felt a chill go down her spine. "So what happened outside by the generator?" She tried again. "You had to defend yourself?"

"Yes, yes, that's what it was: self-defence. You are not too stupid for a cop."

"I'm not a cop. I'm a consultant."

"Whatever." Judith Holland turned around in irritation when the security guard moaned. "Shut up!" She put all her anger into the rebuke and fidgeted with the knife. The man let himself slide to the side and the woman calmed down.

"I read the note he gave me and he put it back into his jacket. Then he winked at me. He went outside to the generator. I took a steak knife off the meat table and put it in my sleeve to hide it and followed him. Bastard! Of course I couldn't let him live or he'd do it over and over again. But I never used it. It would have been self-defense, though..." She sniggered and shrugged her shoulders.

So the pink notes had been written by the lawyer and not by Judith Holland…

"When I got to the generator, he was kind of hanging there. Dead, of course. There was no need for the knife. God had taken care of that one."

So Julius Mandel had electrocuted himself by writing on the faulty plastic pipe, but the woman had still killed at least three victims.

"He would have been dead either way," Charlie confirmed.

"Like hell could I let him do that to me. I worked too hard. Too damn hard to turn my life around and I can't take something like that lying down. Not anymore."

"Who did it before?"

"Wouldn't you like to know?" Judith asked suspiciously.

Oh dear, Charlie thought, but she kept the recording going.

"Might as well tell me the whole story."

"True, you won't get a chance to tell anybody else anyway when I'm done with you. Don't take it personal, but I need to protect my interests."

"Of course I won't take it personal." What else

could Charlie say?

"Well, Simoné at res had found out what I was doing. She'd seen me in one of the clubs in Sunnyside and asked me sneakily what I'd been doing there. I was in shock. If she knew then the other girls would know in no time. She didn't survive the night. I hadn't planned to stab her, but I couldn't allow this to happen."

Judith Holland had murdered a student in Pretoria? This case was getting out of hand. It brought the tally of victims to four so far. Chilling.

"So, no one else found out about Sunnyside?"

"No, not at res. But then, at my old job, it was hell all the same. Nobody knew about my past, but I was told that I'm too nice. Helene and Mahendra were constantly on my case. When I complained that everybody dumped their work on me, my manager wouldn't back me up. I couldn't take it any longer. I resigned. I actually resigned. One dead body was enough, I thought. But I was wrong."

"Bad luck followed you around, then?" Charlie tried to sound empathetic.

"I must be cursed or jinxed or something. My

dreams were going down the drains, because of these people? But I don't give up that easily. This nonsense had to end. I had to make things right for the company and for myself. And I did. It was so natural. Hannah turned her back to me. She asked me if I wanted something to drink. Can you imagine?" Judith sniggered again.

"The nerve of her," Charlie said but thought to herself, you are crazy, lady. Was there more to come?

"I'll say. As if I was there to relax. I saw the knife sticking out from a block of wood. It was the knife with the red hilt. It kind of called to me. I took the knife. It felt different from the first time. Simoné was so thin that the knife just crunched past her bones."

She scoffed at the memory of her first murder.

"Hannah had a lot more bacon on her ribs," she giggled. "The knife went through smoothly like butter. I knew she was dead. Must have hit her heart. That cold and cruel heart of hers. She didn't make a sound that bitch. I don't know how I managed to throw her over the railing, but I did. I think that God gave me the strength. It wasn't nice, but she deserved it. I went downstairs and wiped the hilt of the knife off. Fingerprints, you know…"

"Yes, of course… fingerprints." Charlie thought about what Judith had told her. She must have hoisted her over the balcony quite quickly, because CSI hadn't found much blood in the apartment. Judith Holland was robust, but not exactly Arnold Schwarzenegger. Her desperation must have given her the strength.

"You judge me," the woman said suspiciously. "Ah well, who wouldn't? You probably have a cushy life. Only someone, who went through all of my pain can understand what it's like to be treated that way."

Charlie cringed on the inside. Her life had been fraught with difficulty at times, but she could not imagine what it felt like to be so angry to start killing those, who had done you wrong. In that respect, Judith Holland was right: she couldn't understand.

"I wouldn't say cushy - just different," she replied. "You must have been very upset." She had to keep her talking. Lerato, where are you?

"That doesn't even begin to describe it," Judith hissed.

"What did the receptionist do to you?"

"Who?"

"The man, who worked at the reception, John Bhengu," Charlie clarified. "He was stabbed in the parking lot."

"Oh yes, Bhengu. I saw him talking to Mandel then he looked at me and laughed. I know they were talking of me, of my past. They kept talking and laughing and he looked at me, while I was waiting for the others to go to action cricket practice. They were late, the team. I hate being late. That's why I was early. Julius Mandel left and I asked Bhengu to help me look at my car. He came along... the fool. I don't remember how it happened, but I pushed him and felt so free. It was getting easier now. He would never laugh at me again."

She had killed the married father of two because she'd assumed that the two men had laughed at her. Judith Holland had evidently driven herself mad. She'd started imagining things and John Bhengu had paid the price as well.

"Didn't you have blood on you?" Charlie asked. "You know after you killed John Bhengu."

"Sure, but our company shirts are dark red. It just looked like a few wet spots. In any case, who could tell the difference in the dark?" In summer it was still getting dark in the evening at around 18:30. Bad luck for the receptionist.

"Where did you find the knife to kill him and what did you do with it afterwards?" Charlie asked.

"What do you care?" Judith snapped.

"I'm just curious."

The woman thought for a moment then grinned.

"It took a trip on top of a large truck down on the highway. I watched it go east for a little while before I went back and waited at the entrance for the cricket team. These buggers were fifteen minutes late. We nearly lost our pit at the action cricket place to another team. Anyway… one more problem solved." She giggled again.

"But you weren't quite done yet." Charlie covertly checked her phone.

"No I wasn't and I'm still not." Judith Holland chuckled and Charlie froze.

I beg to differ, she thought. She would do anything in her power to stop this madwoman from hurting anyone else or her. This woman had absolutely no conscience, no empathy. What was taking the police so long?

"Julius Mandel took the exit all by himself, but you can surely see that he had to go as well. As long as he was around, I would not have any peace. I would have been his slave, helping him to defraud the company and going back to being a prostitute? No way," Judith said with determination. "I had no idea that it would be raining so hard during the thunderstorm, but it didn't hurt, did it? "

"Well, you didn't have to use the knife," Carlie answered and couldn't see herself ask these questions much longer.

"Oh really?" Judith Holland asked with a mean look in her eyes.

That's when Charlie finally sent the recording to Lerato's phone.

"What are you doing there?"

"Nothing."

Charlie sweated bullets, but the woman was more concerned with telling her story.

Chapter ELEVEN

"David also paid for disrespecting me," she continued with a sneer and sat down on one of the workstation desks. Was she finally relaxing?

Charlie fumbled with the phone in her pocket, but without being able to look at it, she couldn't get the recording going again.

"Who's David?" She inquired, suddenly feeling cold.

Perhaps he was another colleague Judith had encountered in the stairway when running from the polygraph test? Had she gagged him and tied him up as well? Maybe it was a relative or friend.

It took the woman some time to answer, while her face displayed a variety of emotions. Charlie waited patiently.

"David's my boyfriend… well, my ex-boyfriend now…" Judith eventually said and giggled.

Charlie just nodded. She knew about David, the ex-boyfriend, of course. His younger sister had a holiday job at MultoPharm that Judith Holland had organised at David's request. A callous request under the circumstances.

They had spoken to his sister on the weekend and found out about the details of recent events and that her brother had suddenly broken up with Judith Holland. She had, quite understandably, been heartbroken by the breakup and his decision to take another woman to New Zealand with him.

What had happened to the man? How had he paid for his ill-advised behaviour? Charlie feared the worst but decided to take a chummy tone with the serial killer to get to the truth.

"Men can be such pigs," she agreed with her as convincingly as possible. "He had it coming. How did you make him pay?" A faint rose colour appeared behind the computer monitor. Oh no, Charlie thought.

"You Americans have a different attitude to that sort of thing, don't you?" Judith suddenly changed the subject. "I've watched quite a few episodes of that new police drama…"

"Oh, but I just grew up in America… I'm actually South African."

"One of those chickens, who run away from this

country," Judith Holland said with a suspicious tone in her voice. "Just like David. He should never have done what he did!"

"I agree he shouldn't." Charlie sounded convincing enough.

Why didn't the police come, already? It took the woman another minute to start talking about the details and they were chilling, indeed.

"Ah, that was easier than I thought. He brought some toys around – for his cat. Had a cheek to ask me to take care of her, because nobody in Pretoria wanted to take that fat furball." Judith Holland snorted with contempt. "I walked up to him, said I wanted to speak about our separation… that I needed closure. Cried a few tears," She laughed. "He went for it and turned his back for just a second…"

This murderous woman actually laughed. A deep throaty laugh that made Charlie shudder. She didn't know how much more of this she could take.

Her friend Lerato, who was the actual PI, normally conducted the interviews. Charlie was the one, who usually picked up on clues that were not obvious to others. But this was the first time that Charlie had to get to the truth all by herself and she hated every minute of it.

"He turned his back to me that fool! He never suspected a thing."

"I bet he didn't." Charlie was getting desperate now for something to happen.

Where was the police? She pushed down with her finger where she thought the recorder would switch on. Was it working?

Please let it be on record! She thought. *I can't do this on my own.*

There was no help from the other side either, just reddish colour rising here and there. Charlie was on her own. So she just listened to the disturbing story of how Judith had made David pay for his deceit and wished she could just disappear.

"I thought he would be my forever-partner," Judith said with disdain. "I mean we had plans together. We were planning our married life. Then he drops me just like that, like a hot potato, and wants to make off to New Zealand with his new floozy. Irma, daughter of family friends. I mean, that name alone. He thought they were better suited to each other and his family thought so too. Just like that? Not on my watch… what, I give you the best years of my life and you just drop me for her? Overnight? He never had a chance to take her to New Zealand."

There it was again, that unnerving, throaty laugh.

"You are so smart," Charlie flattered her. The killer might be more amenable if she remained on her side. "Not many would have the guts to do that. And nobody heard a thing?"

Judith Holland pondered this for a moment. She seemed to listen to something and grinned. Then she spoke decisively.

"No, I don't think so. Not the neighbours at least. He never made a noise with all the blood in his mouth. Pushed him away before he could drip it all over me. He wriggled around a few times on the couch then he lay still. I must clean the couch and the carpet now. That pig. I should have poisoned him, but it was more fun that way." She grew serious. "Just so messy to use a knife."

"Right, too bad the carpet's dirty now," Charlie encouraged her.

"Yes. His cat came in and kept meowing. How that

fat ugly thing knew what was happening ... made short shrift of her, too. One kick against the wall was enough to stop that meowing. Then I felt better. Much better. Changed my clothes, washed the blood off, put the knife in a plastic bag and went off to work. Well, to redo the dumb test, rather."

So the knife she was holding had been used in stabbing her ex-boyfriend.

"Yes, the polygraph test," Charlie said and couldn't help but shiver, despite the warm weather. This stabbing had taken place only this morning. A few hours ago. Was her ex-boyfriend David dead?

The answer came in the shape of more vapour that swirled around behind the accountant. Angry, sad vapour. It stopped swirling and settled on one of the desks. The faint shape of a young man formed, as he sat there looking confused.

Where was everybody? It couldn't take them that long to find the right time... *Pull yourself together*, she thought intently.

Thankfully, Judith had lowered the knife, while relating the murder that had taken place only a few hours ago. The security guard began moaning again and Judith Holland turned around knife in hand, ready to rebuke the poor man.

At that moment, the office door opened with a loud crash and police officers came swarming into the office. A rubber plant in a pot next to the whiteboard fell over. They split into small groups and took charge of the situation.

Charlie closed her eyes and took a deep breath.

At last!

She opened her eyes again and saw Lerato nodding at her. Charlie nodded back and got out of the way. She joined her friend underneath the wall clock. Lerato put an arm around Charlie's shoulders. "Thanks for the recordings, she said. They gave us a good idea of how to approach."

"So it worked? But what took you so long? I was slowly dying in here."

"Sorry… we had to wait. Marius requested a negotiator but he's still on his way. Probably stuck in traffic. We couldn't wait any longer."

They paid attention to the fracas in front of them. One of the officers made a dash for the security guard to release him from his restraints. He ripped the duct tape off his mouth and the man jumped at the pain, then breathed in deeply.

"Slow down," the officer said to Herbert Tuins. "Breathe slowly."

The killer, on the other hand, swayed around in the most awkward manner and resisted the hands reaching for her. More officers joined the rumpus but were unsuccessful in restraining her.

Inspector Karen van der Merwe pointed her gun at the serial killer and yelled. "Drop that knife on the floor. Hands up! Get down on your knees. On your knees!"

When Judith Holland realised that the game was up, the look on her face was indescribable.

Her face seemed to melt into an ugly mask of hatred and despair and, instead of complying with the order, the accountant lifted her hand and bared her teeth. Charlie watched in horror how Judith tried to slash her knife at the officers in a flurry of movements, her face in a wild grimace.

She screamed obscenities as she stabbed and slashed away into the air. There was nothing they could do to stop the deranged woman. The officers ducked and dived out of range but she grazed a young policeman's cheek.

She slowed down and taunted him waving her knife. "Come get me…"

Before the accountant could do any more harm, two of the officers dashed in her direction and finally overpowered her. One of the policewomen lay on top of her writhing body and kept knocking her right hand while holding her wrist. The knife flew against one of the computer screens and rattled onto the desk.

The killer stared at the knife, ready to retrieve her weapon but it was out of reach.

She couldn't believe her game was up for good, after all she'd been through.

Her face said it all: her life was over.

Suddenly, the woman screamed and screamed. Mad and sheer uncontrollable, she kicked out over and over again and kept biting into the fabric of the police uniforms. Like a wild animal about to be captured and led to the slaughter. It was disturbing and almost pitiful to watch.

Surely, all those police officers would be able to restrain this writhing madwoman.

Then there was only the shouting of commands

and yelling from officers and the screaming by the woman. When it got all too much, Charlie closed her ears with her hands but couldn't stop watching.

She cringed when one of the policemen got a powerful kick on his shin. The pain caused him to drop the woman's hand he was about to shackle and before anybody could grab hold of her again, Judith Holland had thrown off the policewoman on her back and worked her way up and onto her feet.

The handcuffs clattered to the floor. It was unbelievable. Everything happened so fast that the officers had no time to react.

Once she realised that she was free, the woman looked up and sprinted toward the large windows, banging against one of the desks and shoving a policeman out of the way. Charlie couldn't believe what she was seeing. How could she be so strong?

Judith reached the windows with an astonishing speed and opened the unlocked door to the balcony. Here, smokers spent a few minutes outside every day during coffee breaks, inhaling the smoke of their lit cigarettes come rain or shine.

She had always hated the smoke that wafted into

the office when they opened the door but none of this mattered now. She knew that the door was open and that it was her only way out of the room and the embarrassing defeat.

She had to get away from it all. Had to get away…

"Don't do it." Karen van der Merwe yelled. She stood with her weapon drawn but it had proved to be useless in all of this chaos. "No!"

The moment Judith reached the balcony she was already on top of the railing, scaled over and flung herself headlong two storeys down with an insane scream.

The officers, who had run after her couldn't stop the fall and watched helplessly as she disappeared from view. Charlie didn't dare breathe. For a split second, time seemed to stand still.

They heard the woman crash onto the glass roof that covered the area in front of the reception and the glass roof had broken her fall. Everything went silent then loud shrieks echoed off the walls downstairs and the sound of breaking glass ripped through the air.

Had Judith Holland broken her neck when she hit the large glass awning below? There were more frightened screams and shards of glass shattering on the paving.

That's when everyone started to move again. Some police officers congregated onto the balcony in a bid to assess the situation, while others ran down the stairs.

"There are people waiting by the reception," Lerato said.

Marius Vorster took charge of the upstairs proceedings, while Karen van der Merwe and Johan Phaladi followed the other officers down to the ground floor.

Charlie stood in a daze, unsure whether she should feel empathy or relief or fear.

She didn't notice that Inspector Vorster gave her a worried look once in a while.

The strange conversation she'd had with Judith Holland flashed through her mind. This woman had gone through so much to make it in an unforgiving world and in her profession, only to step into another hellish scenario and lose her mind.

Being asked to cook the books and blackmailed into almost having sex with the one person, who knew her past.

Although she had tried her best, she was unable to remove the stains of her past. Seeing the only way out of her anguish by killing those, who were responsible for the pain and frustration she was feeling. And also some completely innocent ones. Killing, just killing to express her pain.

Now, this was how it would all end?

Charlie couldn't help but feel sorry for this tormented soul, forgetting for a moment that she could have easily been her next victim. She cried and Lerato held her a bit closer.

Somebody led the security guard out through the damaged office door. He could barely walk and the officer held him up by placing his shoulder under his armpit. Herbert Tuins' only crime had been a faulty test result and waiting his turn in the hall outside the little windowless office where Judith Holland had completely lost her mind.

"You okay?" Lerato asked, gently shaking Charlie's shoulder.

"What happened to her?"

"Somebody says that she seems to be alive but there isn't much hope."

"Such a sad story," Charlie mumbled. "She never got a real chance, you know."

"Come, let's get out of here. There's an ambulance downstairs. Let them have a look at you."

Lerato guided Charlie gently down to the parking lot, where the paramedics were seeing to the injured security guard. They also treated some of the staff members for cut wounds. They had been waiting in the reception and were injured when glass shards started flying.

An operation was underway to get Judith Holland down from the shattered glass roof. Blood was dripping from the steel construction that held up her body and Charlie looked away, thinking of how the woman had described the killings of her ex-boyfriend and his cat.

All the other murders must have been just as gruesome and bloody.

Three policemen were doing their best to climb up two ladders to retrieve her body dead or alive as it may be, while two paramedics with a stretcher and other equipment shouted instructions up in case she was still alive.

"Come this way, madam," a paramedic approached them and sat Charlie down on a low wall. He examined her for a few minutes.

"You just have a minor shock. Take a rest and have something to drink."

"Oh good, so I don't have to go to the hospital?" Charlie inquired.

"No, you are good to go. Here, drink this." He handed her a bottle with a light blue liquid. An energy drink.

"She can't have all this sugar," Lerato told the man. "She has an insulin problem."

Lerato handed the bottle back to the paramedic and he put it on the low wall.

"Oh I see, sorry. I suppose a bottle of water will do."

He scrunched around in the ambulance vehicle and produced a small water bottle. Charlie obediently drank the water and Lerato found a sachet of peanuts in her bag.

"Here, eat this," she ordered Charlie.

The security guard lay on a stretcher. He had been wrapped in bandages and a drip was attached to his arm. Herbert Tuins had lost a fair amount of blood while being kept captive by the crazed accountant and would be taken to hospital in the company van. He was in a stable condition and there was no room in the ambulance for two injured persons – unless a mortuary vehicle had to be called.

The van left. The sooner he could get to the hospital, the better.

The killer, who still lay prostrate on a shattered glass roof, was sliding to one side as the police and paramedics shouted and did their best to move her and keep her alive. They were able to stop the bleeding and strap her to the stretcher that was now lowered down onto the paving.

"Okay, got it," one of the policemen shouted and grabbed the lower end of the stretcher. "Take her down. Slowly. slowly, I said."

The woman was not a pretty sight. She had suffered many cuts and her neck was put into a broad collar. Although she was a ruthless murderer, she was treated with dignity. The paramedics worked on her for twenty minutes before she could be transferred to the ambulance vehicle. That meant she was still alive!

Charlie took another swig of the water and began to feel better.

Somebody told John Buitendacht, the CEO of the company, to get out of the way. He was trying to take charge of the operation and was making a nuisance of himself.

A policewoman led the protesting CEO to the side, while Marius Vorster picked his way past the workers who cleaned away glass shards and bloodstains in front of the company building.

"Are you feeling better?" The inspector asked Charlie and sat down next to her.

"The paramedic says I'll be fine, just shaken a bit and rehydrating now." She showed him the half-empty water bottle.

"That's good, I'm glad," he answered. "I was so worried and traffic was a nightmare. We tried to get here as quickly as possible but even the sirens and blue light didn't make much of a difference."

"It's alright," Charlie said. "I'm still here. I hope the recording helped."

"Much. I've seen a lot but this woman's rage was something else."

The seasoned inspector shook his head.

"Hell hath no fury like a woman scorned," Lerato

mumbled.

"How can Judith Holland still be alive after such a fall?" Charlie asked Marius.

"I don't know. I've never seen anything like it."

Charlie saw now several swirls of vapour pouring down from the balcony Judith Holland had taken her jump from.

"Maybe somebody tried to make sure that she doesn't die."

"Oh?" Lerato didn't immediately understand what her friend was talking about.

"I can see four separate vapours next to her. Maybe that's what's keeping her alive," Charlie explained. "Her victims. They must have prevented her suicide."

"You mean they want to see justice done?" Marius Vorster asked.

He had never really believed in supernatural circumstances but this case was just too unusual to ignore the possibility of something supernatural at work.

"Or maybe see her suffer. I can't say for sure." Charlie shrugged her shoulders.

"That doesn't sound good."

"Not good for her, I think." Charlie sighed.

"Well, she did a lot of harm. If she recovers, she'll have to stand trial but that's unlikely if she's severely crippled by her injuries," Marius explained. "She deserves to be tried in a court of law."

"Either way, they'll have their revenge," Lerato stated.

"Yes, they will." Charlie chewed on some peanuts and finished the water in her bottle.

"Well, if you'll excuse me," Inspector Vorster said and walked up to the vehicle of the CSI team that had just arrived at the gate.

The technicians would start working in the room with the polygraph machine.

It took the ambulance another ten minutes to leave the MultoPharm premises with its blue lights flashing, while shaken workers kept collecting the glass and cleaned the blood splatters from the paving under John Buitendacht's close watch.

Chapter TWELVE

When the police entered Judith Holland's apartment, they found a dead ginger cat propped against the wall by the TV set and the body of David Coetzee, lying face down on the outdated couch.

A kitchen knife was stuck in David Coetzee's back and he was drenched in blood. They had obviously arrived too late.

One of his arms was hanging off the edge of the couch, barely touching the floor.

The couch was soaked in blood that had dripped in a fine trickle from his fingers onto the carpet before congealing into a dark-red mess. It was obvious that the man had been unaware of the immediate danger and the furniture was undisturbed.

There were no signs of a struggle, but the disturbing state of the pet that had been smashed violently against the wall and the state of the murder victim were enough to see how angry the outwardly placid accountant must have been.

Hell hath no fury like a woman scorned.

The coroner would later confirm that the kitchen knife had entered David Coetzee's back with such force that it had nearly severed his heart in two.

Inspector Karen van der Merwe, who was leading the squad, put on a pair of silicon gloves and turned the stiffening body on his side.

The brown eyes in his pale face were still wide open in surprise and his open mouth showed blood-stained teeth. Not a pretty sight but the inspector had seen worse. She let the body slide back into the position they had found him in. CSI would take care of the rest.

"I hope that's the last victim we'll find," she said.

"Look at that…" one of the police officers said. He pointed to a pile of half-burned photographs in a large bowl on the coffee table. The photographs showed mainly the victim, Mr. Coetzee, with various other people. A glass frame lay smashed next to the bowl on the table. It was apparent that the ex-girlfriend had finally had enough.

Karen van der Merwe couldn't help but empathise with her anger. She'd had her share of bad relationships in the past but going on a killing spree – that was extreme. She looked back at the man on the couch.

The accountant's first victims had had nothing to do with this man or the sudden breakup but it couldn't have helped the woman's volatile mental state. Now at least four people and a cat were dead. How tragic.

*

Judith Holland on the other hand was still alive in ICU at the hospital - if barely.

It was still touch and go. Her back was broken in several places and she had suffered internal injuries but her suicide bid had failed. The murderer's heart was going strong and although she'd been put in an artificial coma, her brain was functioning at normal levels.

Her arms and legs were also broken and, according to the doctors, she would never walk again or even move her arms. Not a positive prospect under any circumstances.

How this serial killer would live out her days with so much hatred and bitterness inside her was anyone's guess. It would take years for her mangled body to heal and rehabilitate and she would be dependent on the care of others for the rest of her life.

Much to the displeasure of the victims' families, who had hoped to get their revenge in court. But it was unlikely that a trial was going to take place.

The murderer's suffering wouldn't bring their loved ones back.

"I knew it," David Coetzee's mother commented bitterly when a reporter asked her questions for an article in the local newspaper. "I knew that there was something wrong with her all along. We didn't know about her sordid past, of course, but she was always so strange. Smiling, in a good mood, you know, even when she should have been unhappy. I mean most people are unhappy sometimes. And now my son is gone and all our hopes and dreams with him."

She cried into a paper tissue and the reporter gave her a few minutes to compose herself. After dabbing her eyes, she was ready to answer more questions.

"So, you say that Judith Holland had displayed unusual behaviour long before she committed the murders?" The reporter asked.

"I mean, who is always in a good mood?" It was a rhetorical question. "And my son didn't want to listen. Not to his father, not to me. She had him wrapped around her little finger of course. With sex, I'm sure. We had no idea how she'd earned her money as a student. And now it's all over the news. We were so happy when he started seeing Irma. She's a good girl… poor Irma. She's heartbroken like all of us. There will be no wedding and I will never have grandchildren from my only son."

The reporter switched her recording device off. She'd heard enough.

*

'So, how is Johan's nose doing?' Charlie inquired when she spoke to Lerato on the phone. They'd been chatting about this and that for over half an hour.

'Much better, I think. It doesn't seem to bother him anymore. He's coming to the braai tomorrow, with his wife. I met her briefly. She's really nice.'

Charlie and Jono had organised a bring-and-braai for their friends. Everybody would bring what they wanted to barbecue, salads and drinks.

It was the favourite summer pastime of South Africans, spending time in the outdoors and grilling food. Tomorrow, they would sit around the fireplace at the back of the garden after dark. That's the best they could do with yet another electricity blackout looming.

Jono walked into the kitchen, while Billie and Popcorn chased a huge moth. The hapless moth tried to get to the candle on the table that Jono had lit and the dogs kept jumping up to play with its flapping wings.

The power failure had begun at 20:00 and it was dark now. There would be no showers tonight if the electricity didn't come on soon. The geyser needed to heat the water for at least an hour to last for the two of them.

"Dang!" Jono said and tried to catch the moth, while Charlie continued to speak to Lerato on the phone.

Lerato had given Charlie the latest news on the MultoPharm case. Judith Holland was still alive and recovering from her extensive injuries and the court case was still hanging over the company's reputation. The murders didn't make things any better and their international share price had tumbled. The employees were receiving counselling but it would take a while to forget the events of the last few weeks.

'Johan said he'll bring lamb chops. His brother has a farm in the Free State and he gets fresh lamb for Christmas. Not so many TV dinners over Christmas for him and his wife, I hope. They'll go and visit family for a few days in Bloemfontein.'

'That's good and I'm glad he's doing better,' Charlie said. 'I haven't heard from him since that day at MultoPharm…'

'Everybody is trying to forget that day. He's been busy, I guess. Took off only a couple of days from work and is now on the case of a child that was found murdered in the bushes outside of Ennerdale. Among others,' Lerato explained. 'Karen took over the MultoPharm case and the report should be out soon.'

'Thank goodness that's done and dusted. Creepy and rather unhelpful spirits to boot with.' Jono looked at her and grinned. Charlie thumped him on the arm. 'Heard about the Ennerdale case. So sad. I'm glad they didn't call us in to help solve the murder. It was the uncle, wasn't it?'

'Yes, a pillar of society. Yuck! A pretty straightforward case. A slam-dunk for once, so no need for us to help the police. Child murders are the worst. Let's rather talk about the braai tomorrow. At what time do you want us to be there?' Lerato asked.

'Oh, is Peter coming, too? I thought he had to go to Durban on business.'

'They postponed the trip to the beginning of next year at the last minute. I'm glad we can spend Christmas together in Joburg.'

Charlie agreed. 'That's great. I'm glad for you. Peter's been travelling a lot lately.'

'So when do you want us to be there?'

'Well, we thought that 4 o'clock would be a good time to start.'

'4 o'clock is perfect. I'll go to Woolies just now as soon as I'm done with my paperwork and buy some chips and dip, chicken pieces and a ready-made salad.'

'Sounds good. Are the boys taking care of the cut wood and the charcoal?' Charlie asked. 'We haven't really discussed it.'

'I hope so…' Lerato answered.

"Jono, did you buy the charcoal and cut wood for the braai tomorrow?" Charlie turned around to ask her brother, who'd managed to catch the unwilling moth and was busy placing it on the bougainvillaea bush outside by the driveway.

"No, not yet. I'll do it in the morning. We'll need a few bags of wood for the fireplace as well. The forecast is 30%, I just hope we won't get rain."

"I hope so, too. 30% usually means no rain," Charlie said in an upbeat tone.

The memory of the MultoPharm Christmas party popped into her mind. It was not something Charlie wanted to relive.

This Christmas party was going to be very different. Her late husband Colin had never been to South Africa but he would have enjoyed the warm weather over December and a good barbecue.

'Lerato?' Charlie went back to her phone call. 'Jono says he'll do it tomorrow morning, so don't worry.'

'Done. I'll see you tomorrow at 4 o'clock, then.'

'Righto. Bye for now.'

Charlie and Jono had takeaway dinner that evening. Chinese takeaway always arrived quickly. At least the restaurant at the shopping centre had a generator.

It was late when the electricity came back on. Too

late for a hot shower.

*

"No Popcorn, that's not for you. Sit down… good boy," Jono reprimanded the little white poodle. "Here Peter, could you put the chicken on the braai?"

"Sure." Peter, Lerato's boyfriend took the plate with the marinated chicken thighs from Jono and began to place them with a tong on the hot grill.

Braaing was a man's job. The women were sitting around the table in the shade under the large tree. A jug of ice tea sat in the middle of the table and a couple of bowls with potato chips. Johan's wife was a pleasant young woman, whose face lit up in a smile whenever she looked at her husband.

They had been married just over a year and were obviously very happy.

Karen van der Merwe had also joined them for a few hours. She would be off soon to see her parents. Tomorrow she would take them to Pretoria for the big family Christmas lunch.

"Oh, I like that song," Charlie said. The women made subtle dance-moves while sitting in their chairs. "REM is one of my favourites."

The sun was already beginning to dip behind the neighbour's roof and in about two hours darkness would set in over Johannesburg. If the load-shedding schedule could be trusted, electricity would go off at about that time.

South Africans were taking it all in their stride.

"I'll get the boerewors. Do you want another beer?" Jono asked Johan.

The police inspector seemed in good spirits. "No, thanks I think I'll stick to cool drinks. It's pretty hot today. Probably still around 30 degrees. Can't afford to get drunk. Police inspector or not, if they catch me driving with any alcohol in my blood, I'll be in deep trouble."

"I can drive," his wife tried to help him out. "If you want to drink, you have my permission to do so." She smiled as she looked at him.

"Thanks love but I'd rather not," he said.

"As you wish, Johnny." She called him Johnny and Charlie thought it rather cute.

"But it seems to be cooling down now," Jono said. "Alright, one diet coke coming up for Inspector Phaladi. It'll be cool enough to start the fire in the pit soon. Thanks for putting the paper and wood in so long."

They were planning to sit around the fire pit with drinks later and ride out the couple of hours of load-shedding.

"My pleasure." Peter continued to place and move around chicken pieces on the hot metal grid. "You've got lots of twigs lying around. We'll have a fine fire."

Jono walked past the table on the way to the kitchen. He was wearing a red and white felt Santa hat, and so was Peter.

"Wait I'll come with you. Need to make more ice tea." Charlie followed her brother down the driveway. "Hope there's still rosella to go with the rooibos teabags. Be right back." Lerato nodded. She was unusually quiet and listening to the music.

"Phew, it's hot. I hope we still have enough ice cubes," she said and placed the empty glass jug on the counter by the door.

"Where's the boerewors?" Jono asked and opened the fridge.

"On the top shelf."

"Ah, I see it. Two packets. Let me take them outside."

"Sure." Charlie prepared the ice tea and hummed

along to the song that was softly playing outside. There was some tension between her and Jono.

Her brother had told her that he'd been on a coffee date with Karen van der Merwe and that he would like to date her. To say that Charlie was shocked was an understatement.

Inspector van der Merwe had been so offish on their double date and she'd seemed to have a bit of a crush on her colleague Marius Vorster rather than her brother Jono.

She hadn't been very nice to Charlie and never in a million years would she have guessed that there had been a romantic spark between the two of them. That just showed you how things could change.

The fact that Jono hadn't told Charlie, left her a bit miffed. It was unusual for the siblings to keep things like that unspoken.

Karen was showing her off-duty side and being quite pleasant today. So far so good.

Considering the inspector's usually harsh behaviour, Charlie felt a sense of protection for her older brother. But he was old enough and had to make up his own mind. He could date whomever he wanted.

She was still not sure about Marius Vorster and they were not dating for sure but she thought of him tenderly. It was also a great thing he had done for Jono. The Police officer, who had tried to get a bribe from her brother had been found and disciplined.

Marius must surely be halfway in Port Elizabeth by now. He was planning to join family members to celebrate Christmas by the beach and was taking his ex-wife and his daughter down to the coast with him.

His ex-wife had broken up with her boyfriend and was now in the picture again. Only for their daughter's sake, Marius had assured Charlie.

Too bad that he wasn't here at their little get-together but having children came with obligations. Charlie understood that.

The cell phone on the kitchen counter vibrated.

Charlie had topped the brewed tea up with cool water and was emptying a tray full of ice cubes into the glass jug. She wiped her hands on her shorts, picked up the phone and placed the jug in the fridge. She was almost done.

Charlie answered, holding the phone awkwardly. 'Hello.'

She heard Karen laughing outside and then Lerato. Her friend always took a little longer before getting a joke.

Charlie could still not believe that the stern policewoman and her brother were dating but she had begun to accept the idea. When Karen laughed, she looked so much younger and happier than she had during their double date at the Piccachu restaurant.

Her thoughts dwelt on all of this, while she took a bottle of Coca Cola out of the fridge to make space for the ice tea. The sugar-free variety. Billie and Popcorn jumped around her.

"Hey you little buggers, don't trip me up!" She laughed. 'Hellooo, helloo,' she said repeatedly.

She didn't recognise the number. Perhaps it was Marius Vorster, who wanted to let her know that he'd arrived safely in Port Elizabeth.

'Hello,' a man said, in a hesitating tone. Charlie picked up a slight accent. Wrong number, maybe. 'Is this Charlotte Papadopoulos?'

This was clearly not Marius Vorster or anybody else she knew.

For some unknown reason, Charlie felt her blood

rush to her head. It made her feel a little dizzy. Who was this man?

'That… that used to be my name a long time ago. Who is this? I'm sorry, but I have guests and I'm not interested in whatever you have to sell…'

'I don't want to sell anything to you.' The man had a strange accent she'd never heard before. Was it German? It sounded German.

'I'm in Johannesburg for the holiday season and I thought I should at least give you a call,' the man said. She couldn't explain the strange feeling she had when he continued speaking.

'Oh, why is that?' Charlie asked. 'Have we met before? In New York?'

'Well you see, my name is Sven Olson and I am your father.'

Charlie nearly dropped the coke bottle she was still holding.

"Really? That's how it is?" She heard Peter shout outside. Then Jono said something and everybody began laughing.

Her father?

This was her father calling her on Christmas?

A million thoughts started swirling in her head and she had to sit down. What did he want?

'Hello… Charlie? Are you still there?'

How dare this man call her by her nickname?

A wave of anger flooded her. Then the anger was faded and a feeling of longing filled her. This was her father, her elusive father she'd longed to meet for so long.

'Yes… Dad. I'm still there.'

The End

THE AUTHOR

Evadeen Brickwood grew up with two sisters in Germany and studied cultural sciences and languages. As a young woman, she travelled extensively and many of her books are inspired by her experiences abroad. Feeling adventurous, the newly qualified translator moved to Africa in 1988 and worked for two years as a secretary and language teacher in Botswana. The author eventually settled in South Africa, where she got married and raised two daughters.

In Johannesburg, Evadeen Brickwood studied computers and management of training and worked as a corporate software trainer, professional translator and lecturer at WITS University. In 2003, she began her writing career with youth novels in the 'Remember the Future' series, about adventures in prehistory. Book 1, the award-winning 'Children of the Moon', has been published twice in South Africa and translated into German. The author now self-publishes and you can look forward to episodes in the new, off-beat Charlie Proudfoot series, which is set in South Africa.

The author's websites are:

http:/www.evadeen.wixsite.com/charlieproudfoot

http:/www.evadeen.wixsite.com/novels

http:/www.evadeen.wixsite.com/youngbooks

Evadeen is looking forward to your mail and can also be contacted on social media, incl. Facebook, Twitter, Instagram, Pinterest, google+ and Goodreads.

ABOUT THIS EPISODE

For many years, I worked in the corporate world and was a leader in organised business. It was in this environment that I witnessed what can happen under the glossy veneer of prestigious firms and government organisation. Not to say that every compay has this culture, but nobody wants to openly talk about these often very real issues.

The accounting profession has the reputation of being for introverts without a sense of humour, as one of the characters in the story describes it. However, I know of a number of accountants, who do not fit at all into this stereotype. You know who you are...

I've also seen moral values dropping like domino pieces when it comes to profits and prestige. In "Glass Ceiling", things go down the rabbit hole of murderous toughts and actions. In the next episode, you can look forward to see how an ill-considered affair can have unwanted consequences.

Evadeen Brickwood

THE NEXT EPISODE
in the Charlie Proudfoot Series

5

MORE BOOKS BY
EVADEEN BRICKWOOD

This adventure mystery tells the story of 22-year-old Bridget Reinhold who is not exactly the adventurous type, but when her sister Claire disappears in Southern Africa, nothing can hold her in England. Bridget launches herself into the search in Botswana and encounters obstacle after obstacle. She learns the basics of the native language and culture and soon moves to the capital city of Gaborone. Soon, her mission is plunged into turmoil as everything seems to be going wrong. Just coincidence or is there something more sinister at work?

Another mystery novel set in modern South Africa. This time, the murders of a ranger and a rare black rhino in the idyllic Shangari Safari Park rattle the local community of Rutgersdrift. Sofia Helenius from Finland lives at the lodge with her boyfriend Tom Rutgers, the owner of Shangari. Sofia is tormented by a secret she yearns to share with Tom, but the cruel events grab the limelight and put everything else in the shade. One of the native Khoi-San families is known to communicate with wild animals, but what if the criminals get wind of this gift?

When another murder happens in the city of Johannesburg, smouldering secrets begin to unravel. How are the murders connected and will it be possible to halt a relentless crime-syndicate in order to save an African paradise?

As if growing up in the seventies wasn't difficult enough, teenager Isabell Bertrand is also too rebellious for her parents' liking. A novel treatment with hypnosis appears to be the perfect remedy and Dr. Albrecht regresses Isabell to her early childhood and even further back. She experiences previous lifetimes and then one in particular: could this beautiful young woman in a silk sari, who was forced to choose between two men, really once have been her? Years later, Isabell is invited to a wedding in Pakistan and memories of a forgotten love come flooding back - with dangerous consequences.

Can you imagine, suddenly living in the past? Not last year or in the Roman Empire, but a really, really long time ago?

Katherine, Trevor and Chryséis embark on a sea voyage and sail across the prehistoric ocean to the remnants of a sunken continent. Suddenly everybody seems to be after a mysterious speaking stone from the fabled land of Lyonesse.

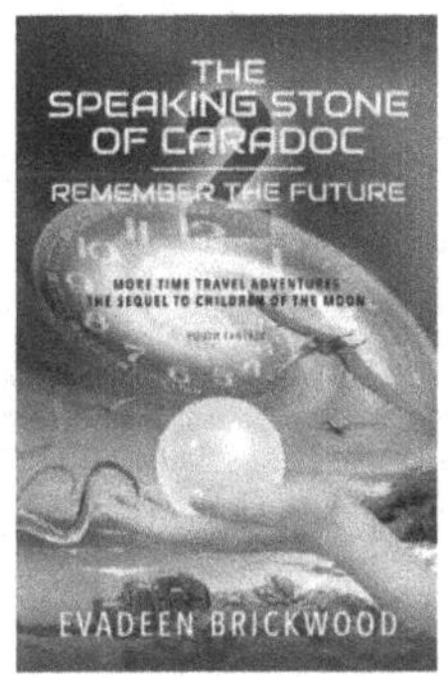

Finding their way back to Alesia and their home in the future, turns out to be more difficult than the time travellers thought. War breaks out in the Mediterranean Sea and forces Katherine, Trevor and Chryséis to flee inland. Nothing here is the way they thought it would be, and who has ever heard of Egypt without pyramids?